© Copyright 2021 by Lilly Wilder All rights reserved.

In no way is it legal to reproduce, duplicate, or transmit any part of this document in either electronic means or in printed format. Recording of this publication is strictly prohibited and any storage of this document is not allowed unless with written permission from the publisher. All rights reserved.

Respective authors own all copyrights not held by the publisher.

Rejected Academy

Wolf Shifter Menage Protector Romance

By: Lilly Wilder

Table of Contents

Foreword

Chapter 1

Chapter 2

Chapter 3

Chapter 4

Chapter 5

Chapter 6

Chapter 7

Chapter 8

Chapter 9

Chapter 10

Chapter 11

Chapter 12

Chapter 13

Chapter 14

Chapter 15

Chapter 16

Chapter 17

Chapter 18

Chapter 19

Chapter 20

Chapter 21

Chapter 22

Chapter 23

Chapter 24

Chapter 25

Chapter 26

Chapter 27

Chapter 28

Chapter 29

Epilogue

Foreword

Outcasts are to be rejected. Shunned. Spurned. Not protected. Yet, I was.

We all knew that my father challenging the Alpha would get us punished. He died doing what he thought was right. My own fate? Sometimes, I think it's worse than death. My mate rejected me. My clan exiled me. I was forced to seek refuge at the Hermitage, the only place for outcast wolf shifters.

Ours is a world of old values. Old magic. Old rules. If you break them, you'd better be ready to pay the price. This is what everyone knows. But what I couldn't have known was that two brothers I meet would end up being my confidants, my protectors, my everything.

Our bond will be stronger than the old ways. It has to be... because my life depends on it.

Rejected Academy

Chapter 1
Cat

I watch with horror as the Alpha digs his bloodstained canines into the body of the wolf lying on the ground, whose every breath could be its last. Its grey hair is entangled with mud and blood. The body whimpers in pain, barely audibly. I can't look away, no matter how much I'd like to. The faces around me are all familiar. Now, that familiarity has transformed into hate, cutting sharp as a knife.

I don't even feel the claws digging into each of my upper arms, rendering me frozen and helpless. It was actually the sight before me which left me paralyzed, not their grip. My entire body is a lump of nerves, and every breath I take makes me twitch painfully.

If I didn't know any better, I'd think this was all just a dream. A horrible nightmare which wouldn't let me open my eyes and wake up into the safety of reality. This is my reality now.

The Alpha spits a piece of flesh onto the dirt before my feet, and I gasp silently. I stare at him, forcing myself not to look away. Above him, the full moon is peeking out from the clouds, like a shiny coin. My mother always told me the moon would guide me, protect me.

The moon is the guardian of all wolves. Just look up to it when you're in need of help, and it will lead you even through the darkest of nights...

My mother's words echo inside my mind like a bell in an empty church, with no one to hear it. Without even glancing up at the moon, I curse it silently. How can it just stand by while my father is being mauled to death? The moon is no friend of mine, no protector. My mother was wrong.

A few moments later, we all witness the Alpha changing back into his human form. The initial, dull pain is evident on his face. We all know it. We've all felt that promise of a torment to come, slithering down one's back, then spreading into the limbs. It always starts slow, almost toying with our hopes that maybe, just maybe it won't hurt as much this time. Only, it always does. It tears us apart from the inside, breaking bone and pulling apart flesh, only to readjust into a new form. Our true form.

Naked and bloody, our Alpha walks up to me, stepping through a puddle of my father's blood. I hold his stare, defiant not to look away even for a single moment.

He bares his teeth in front of me, crystalline and razor-sharp. His arms are long, muscular. His nails are as sharp as his fangs. A dark tuft of fur rests in the middle of his carved chest, a reminder that his true self could emerge once again at any moment and smite me. It would only take one blow. No more than that. I allow myself to drown in the hatred of his stare.

"Let it be known now and forevermore," he starts speaking as if the entire woods were his stage.

In a way, it is so. The Wailing Woods are his playground. Other clans know to keep away from here unless they want to return with a limb too short, if they are allowed to return at all. It is a cold, hard place ruled by an even colder and harder Alpha. My father hoped he could change that, but...

He has warned me this might happen. He told me to control my pain, to steady my breathing, not to lose control no matter what. He believed Kaige won't kill me, but looking into those dark pools of loathing, I'm not so sure.

"Whoever dares challenge me, will meet the same fate as Rumlar!" he shouts, and a loud echo of roaring and howling explodes all around me.

He is a handsome man, more so than many others who are his age. He oozes authority, which is why most wolves fear him instead of respecting him. Kaige doesn't seem to care, as long as he's got everyone under his thumb. Fierce and competitive, all he cares about is power. Not us, not his clan.

He gets into my face so close I can feel the stench of blood on his breath. My father's blood. My hands curl into fists, although there isn't much I can do with them. My teeth grind against each other. The pressure persists, slowly converting into bearable pain. My skin crawls at his presence, at his closeness.

"If you're going to kill me, then get it over with already," I growl at him angrily.

"Kill you?" he looks away at the crowd that's gathered around us. To my right, the fire crackles softly. "I would never kill my sister's child."

The noise dies down, and a few heads turn to the people nearest to them, to whisper something. I manage to catch a glimpse of people I once considered friends, but they look away.

"Tidus!" he shouts at the crowd. "Come forth!"

A young man stumbles forth. He doesn't even look at me. The moon glares from above us, the shadows around us menacing, but not more so than the faces I can actually see.

Tidus stops, unwilling to come closer. His ginger red hair now looks dark, almost black, while his face is illuminated by the firelight. His eyes the color of blossoming woods are hidden beneath his lowered eyelids. His hands are behind his back, his fingers which were more than once intertwined with mine. A distant echo of the words he told me rings inside my mind.

"I usually wouldn't bestow this chance upon the daughter of someone who tried to kill me," Kaige snarls, "but, you are still family. So, I will allow you to take your promised mate with you."

"I don't want to go!" Tidus's voice scrapes against my ears like rusty nails. "Don't make me!"

I watch his sniveling face still unable to look at me. His fear of dying is so strong it reeks. Disgust takes over me, and I can't believe that I ever thought this man could be my mate. Hatred washes over me the likes of which I never thought possible.

"I don't want him," I growl back at Kaige.

I'm going to survive this night. I will do so without any dead weight.

"Suit yourself," Kaige replies, dismissing Tidus with one flippant wave of the hand. "But, remember one thing, Ecaterina. I am not giving you freedom. This is to honor the memory of your late mother, my sister, and it shall not be repeated. If I ever see you again, I will slit your throat with my own teeth, do you understand?"

I don't dignify that with an answer immediately. My nostrils are flaring up at him, hot air oozing out of me like molten lava. I feel like my one breath could smite him.

He gets in my face once more, and I'd like nothing more than to lunge at him with my canines out. But, I know better than to act upon that need. That would only get me killed.

"Do I need to repeat myself?" he snarls.

"No," I manage to squeeze through clenched teeth. "I heard what you said."

"Let her go," he instructs the two men by my side, and suddenly, the grip is gone.

Immediately, I turn around and start running. I don't need to turn around to know that no one is following me. Not this time, at least. I keep running, paying no heed to the fact I'm barely breathing. My own hatred and tears streaming down my face are trying to suffocate me, but I keep going. I need to. There is only one way and that is forward.

Kaige was right. It wasn't the path to freedom, but rather to self-imposed prison. Wherever I end up, I will need to stay there indefinitely.

You say that as if you don't know where you're going, my mind tells me.

I keep running towards the western side of the Wailing Woods. There is dirt and grass underneath my bare feet. Musk and moss. When I reach the Raven Caves, I have to go around, and follow the stream. Fresh water revives me and provides strength to go on, for this will take all night. It will take me out of the Wailing Woods and up the Malefic Mountains. When I finally reach the top, that is where it is. The Hermitage.

It is the only place where outcast wolf shifters can find peace, or any semblance of it. It was established by the first ever pariah, who stumbled onto the ruins of an old monastery. Over the course of following centuries, what he started others have finished, and now, it stands tall, its ancient gates and walls offering shelter to those who have been left shunned and exiled from their own homes.

I never even imagined that I would end up there. It all still seems like a horrible nightmare, but I know it's not. My ears prick up at every sound around me. I'm famished, but I won't hunt. Not now. Instead, I keep climbing the difficult ridge, already seeing the first morning light illuminate the outer walls of the Hermitage.

Jagged rocks slice into my flesh as I keep climbing. I feel like every breath I take is the penultimate one. I still keep going because forward is the only way to go. Going back would mean certain death for me. I drink in the sight before me, the heavy gates propped up with thick lumber. There is no way inside other than through the open gates. It provides some peace of mind. I know I won't be completely safe anywhere, but this is as good as it gets.

When I finally climb up, every subsequent breath feels like a stab in the abdomen. I take a seat, my throat completely dry, despite having drunk from the stream. The thought of that ice cold water makes me feel even worse. I whimper quietly, forcing myself to get up.

"What are you doing here?"

I suddenly hear a voice come from somewhere behind me. I jump to my feet, ready to explain or defend myself, whichever comes first.

Before my eyes fall on the intruder to my solitude, I catch his scent. Their scent. There are two of them. The little, invisible hairs on my back stiffen. Friend or foe – I'm still not sure which they are.

I finally see them. One of them is closer to me. His eyes are bright blue, curiosity glimmering in his gaze. His ruffled, black hair falls to the side of his face. His lower arms are bare, revealing an intricate tangle of healed scars, almost creating a purposeful image. The one next to him has the same gaze, the same jawbone structure, the same forehead.

Brothers?

He inches closer to me, and I see that the man next to him has a basket filled with herbs and mushrooms. I'm still on guard. I don't know if I can trust them or not.

"I seek entrance to the Hermitage," I say.

My stomach reminds me of the merciless hunger threatening to overtake me. I'm on the verge of grabbing that basket and stuffing myself full of mushrooms, even though I know they might not be picked for eating, but rather for making potions and balms. I can't think about that now. I have to figure out what to do.

They both look at me inquisitively, then give each other a meaningful glance. Their eyes fall on me once more, with even more curiosity, and something else, something I can't quite put my finger on.

Just like that, they walk over to me completely doing away with the distance between us, and I don't back down. A flame flickers inside of me. Dare I call it hope? Or, maybe it is something else, something completely different, as I gaze into the eyes of these two men, feeling a strange bond already start to form.

"Come," the first one tells me, smiling. "We'll show you the way."

Chapter 2
Cat

The endless sea of night shadows has disappeared, as I feel my fate separating from the original design, and twisting like rivulets, streaming in strange new directions I know nothing about. I follow the two men in front of me, who don't even turn around to check and see whether I'm following them or not.

I only see the one walking right ahead of me clearly. There is a typical wolf-man handsomeness about him. He is rugged and strong, with intertwined ropes of muscle visible underneath his clothes. His legs are long, made for running of course. Yet, he doesn't run. He walks much faster than I ever could have, especially under the conditions.

My insides hurt. I feel exhausted and weakened by hunger. I barely recognize myself when I glance at a puddle underneath my feet. There is a huge, gaping nothingness inside of me which is only inhabited by hate and a desire for vengeance.

We finally reach a tall wall made of stone. The rocks are so smooth that I doubt even the most skillful climber could reach the top. The first man knocks loudly on the wooden door with his fist. A few moments later, a small window opens, and two curious eyes peer at us.

"We're back," the man says, then turns to me. "And, we found her wandering the woods. She says she wants to join us."

"That's for Taarus to decide," the voice on the other side of the door replies.

The window swiftly closes, and I hear a heavy latch open on the other side, resembling some sort of a machinery. There is a clicking, then loud screeching, and finally, the door opens slowly and heavily, granting us access into what I can only assume is the Hermitage.

The two men walk inside, and I immediately follow. It feels like I've entered into the previous century. The ground underneath my feet is hard. There is barely any dirt, which seems to be piled up in the corners.

A small group of people are already huddling together in small areas of the yard. There is a group by the well, also one by a small garden which seems to be filled with underground vegetables like carrots and potatoes. A small flowerbed rests just before the entrance to the mountain itself.

Their curious looks don't escape me, but I don't see judgment. I don't see hatred nor fear. Maybe it's really true what I've heard of this place. Everyone is the same here. No one is better or worse.

"Try to keep up," one of the two men turns to me.

I just nod and hasten my step. We reach the mouth of a cave, which I can only assume is the entrance to the Maleficent Mountains. I have already forgotten all about the thick forest behind me, as a silent welcome threatens to swallow me whole. The men before me don't hesitate to enter, and neither do I.

The passageway is dark, illuminated by what appear to be hundreds of oil lamps hanging from the sides of the walls, providing enough light for us to see where we are headed. I can barely keep up, after running all night long, and that exhaustion is the only thing which has its arms around me, reminding me of what had happened.

As we continue to walk, I sense the faint smell of mold. Somewhere in the distance, water is dripping. Perhaps there is a source of water coming from inside the mountains as well. I click my lips together at the thought of water.

I have no idea how long we've been walking, when finally, they turn right, and we enter a room that looks like an enormous amphitheater, with the stage set right at the end. The acoustics are amazing. I can hear my own breathing as loudly as if I were talking, so I try to breathe less audibly. We approach an elongated table, at the end of which a man is seated, his eyes seared into mine.

"Taarus," one of the two men addresses the old sage, "we bring a newcomer."

The old man doesn't say anything at first. He stands up, and his old grey beard drops almost down to the floor. His hair is of the same color, and there is as much of it as there is his beard. I wonder if it wouldn't be easier to just chop it all off, but I guess then the wise old wizard look would be gone.

He is wearing a long dark robe falling to the ground, trailing behind him as he approaches me. His eyebrows are thick and bushy, like a roof over his eyes, which are strikingly green, the color of new buds in the spring.

He walks slowly, without the slightest trace of haste. When he finally approaches me, I feel like his very gaze is enough to keep me still, in place. I won't run away. He knows it. I know it. There is nowhere to run to, even if I didn't want to be here.

"There is something familiar about you," Taarus speaks, and his voice envelops me in ancient sounds of yore. His is the voice akin to the first voice that was ever to break the silence of the world without humans.

"I've never been here before," I reply.

"You are a thorn," he tells me.

"A thorn?" I frown.

Only now do I see that his long robe is a dark brown deerskin, held around his waist with a black belt.

"Who did you belong to?" he doesn't reply to my question, just continues with his own. Seeing I am the intruder here, I simply go along with it.

"I am of – " I try to answer, but he lifts his hand right in front of my face, signaling at me to stop talking. So, I do.

He leans closer to me, and inhales so deeply that his breath pulls a few loose curls of my hair to himself. Then, he exhales with his lips parted and his eyes closed, as if he's intaking the very essence of my being, trying to determine my roots.

I doubt anyone can do that just through one sniff. I remain still, reminding myself that nothing and no one in this place should pose a threat to me, but helplessness is a dangerous thing. It makes you act in ways you never thought you'd act before, and right now, it is the only thing I know for sure, the only thing I can rely on.

"You are Rumlar's offspring," he speaks immediately upon opening his eyes.

I feel like shock engulfs me whole, intertwining with the grief and powerlessness I can't seem to run away from. I glance over at the guys. They seem to be used to this weird shaman show. When I came here, I wasn't expecting someone like this. I guess I don't even know who I was expecting. The memory of my father's death is a terror I shall never escape or forget. Maybe I should stop trying to.

"I am Ecaterina, the daughter of Rumlar," I nod, acknowledging the acute pain which is threatening to sear me in half with its might. "In a just world, that is what I would still be. But, this is not a just world. This is not even a good world. And, I am not my father's daughter any longer. I am no one's child."

He doesn't say anything. He doesn't have to. I can read the sympathy in his eyes, but I don't understand it.

"Did you know my father?" I ask as the oil lamps around us cast soft, orange lights.

"In another lifetime, yes," Taarus nods solemnly, turning away from me for a moment. "I am sorry to hear of his death, which I assume did not come naturally."

"Not by a long shot," I spit out, a little more venomously than I intended to.

The guys give me a shocked look, as if they never expected such hatred to exist within such a frame. Well, surprise. Even quiet, tender hearts can burn with hatred the strength of a thousand suns.

"The cause of your arrival here is irrelevant," Taarus suddenly informs me, and impudence explodes within me.

He knew my father. How could he say such a thing, that his death doesn't matter?

"The cause of my arrival is the most important thing in my life," I growl back. "My father is dead. The only life I've ever known has been taken away from me. And, I –
"

"Everyone here has arrived as a result of a tragic occurrence," he interrupts calmly, but that doesn't make me less angry. "You'll learn to control your emotions. You are far too young to possess that skill, especially in the light of current events."

There is no tenderness in his voice, and yet, there is no judgment either. He is merely speaking something that sounds like a prerecorded message. He monologues it to everyone, just rearranges a few bits and pieces to better suit each case.

"I don't want to control my emotions," I say, but it sounds more like the pouting of a child who didn't get his way.

"Then, you do not belong with us," Taarus stares me down, and it takes all my conscious effort not to look away.

"Thanks for nothing!" I snarl, turning away to go, but a hand grips me on the elbow, digging its fingers into my skin.

I tug at my hand, realizing that it's one of the two guys.

"Let me go!" I hiss.

"Don't let your stubborn pride cost you your place here," he whispers, although I'm sure everyone's heard him.

He lets me go, but now, without him pulling me to stay, I can't seem to move my legs. Taarus is with his back turned to me. Something inside of me is urging me to talk, to stay, to fight for my place here, if necessary.

"Two paths are diverging before you," Taarus continues, now with his face to me. His eyes are threatening to drown me. "You may go back the way you came from, although I do not advise that. Or, you may stay with us, which is a choice also not without its repercussions."

"What do you mean?" I frown.

"All shall be revealed to those who possess enough patience," his lips widen into a smile, which is the last thing I expected him to do. "Take her to the Cave of Cleansing."

He waves his hand at the guys, and suddenly, I'm taken back outside, without the slightest explanation what just happened. The sun welcomes me back into its realm, and I relish its warm rays on my pale cheek. The guys are both at my side, and I feel the gentle nudge of two hands one on my elbow, and the other on my lower back.

"Where are we going?" I ask loudly, hoping at least one of them will reply.

We pass the dirt yard, and the huddled groups of people, whose eyes are following us up a flight of stone stairs. There are no safety rails on the side, and I try not to look down, as we keep climbing higher and higher. Finally, after what seems a whole hour of climbing, we reach the very top of the mountain.

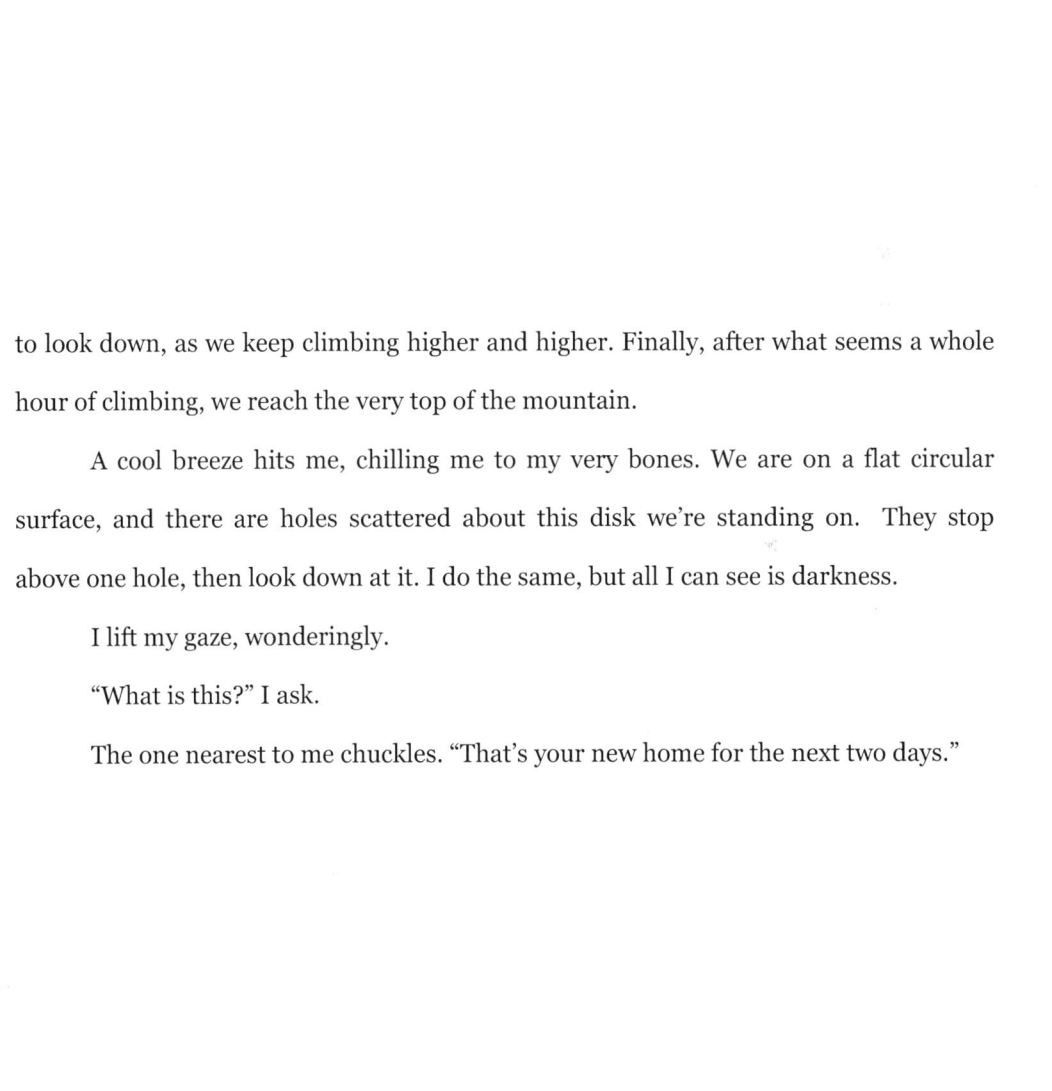

A cool breeze hits me, chilling me to my very bones. We are on a flat circular surface, and there are holes scattered about this disk we're standing on. They stop above one hole, then look down at it. I do the same, but all I can see is darkness.

I lift my gaze, wonderingly.

"What is this?" I ask.

The one nearest to me chuckles. "That's your new home for the next two days."

Chapter 3
Cat

I look around me and all I see is darkness. The only light comes from above me. I let it shine on me, soaking up the sunrays as if I would never see the sunlight again. In a way, that is exactly what this feels like.

I look up. The guys are looking down at me. The rope I used to climb down is gone. They've taken it away, and with it all chances of getting out of this hole. A part of me doesn't want to do this. Why do I have to prove myself? Haven't enough bad things happened to me already? Do I really need to undertake yet another to prove that I deserve to be here?

"You can still change your mind," I hear one of them tell me.

"You know, I still have no idea which one of you is doing the talking, since I don't know your names," I reply a little annoyed.

My neck becomes stiff, so I lower my gaze. I hear a soft chuckle from somewhere up above.

"You're right. That is the first thing we should have done," I hear a reply. "I'm Stefan. And, this is my brother Vlad."

I look up again. "Like Dracula?"

Vlad chuckles again... I'm guessing.

"Exactly like that," he confirms.

"I suppose being in this cave wouldn't bother you then," I say, in a concealed effort to keep them here with me as long as possible.

I still have no idea if they are here to help me, but for some reason, I don't want them gone. I don't want to be all alone again.

"Why not?" Vlad wonders, looking down.

"You could turn into a bat and just fly away," I remind him. "Wish I could do the same."

"But, where would you fly off to?" Stefan asks.

The sun is high up in the clouds right above them, and their faces are veiled in shadowy darkness.

"You're right," I sigh. "Nowhere. There is nowhere to go, nowhere to be."

"There is here," Stefan adds. "You just have to spend a day or two in this cave."

"I won't find a monster hiding in the darkness, will I?" I ask as a joke, but the darkness feels too menacing not to consider this possibility.

I wonder how dark it will get during the night. My eyes open or closed – it probably won't make any difference. The obscurity will be the same.

"Only yourself," Vlad answers this time.

"We'll come see you in the evening, before it gets completely dark down there."

"Can't I have a candle or something?" I frown.

"Then it wouldn't be much of a cleansing, now would it?" Vlad chuckles again. "Just... talk to yourself when you feel uneasy. It helped me."

With those words, they pull away and I can't see them any longer. Alone once again, I feel the exhaustion wash over me, so I sit down on the cold, damp floor. I want to lean against a wall, but I don't want to move away from the light source.

A part of me wonders if this is some kind of a trap. Maybe this isn't the Hermitage at all, but some completely other place, and they've lied to me. They've trapped me here and now, all they need to do is send word to Kaige, so he can come and do away with me. I doubt he cares anymore that I am his late sister's daughter.

I take a deep breath, and the exhaustion is so overpowering that I feel like every single muscle in my body hurts. I lift up my knees and rest my head on them. Cave of Cleansing. It feels like a cave prison more than a cave of cleansing. I wonder how long I need to stay here. A day? Two? What if something happens and they forget about me? What if I never leave this place and I'm sentenced to die looking at the sky?

I feel the overpowering urge to eat something, anything. Even the dirt around me. It's an old and untold hunger I'm feeling, the likes of which I've never felt before. Perhaps that is the start of the cleansing process. My spine tickles with sensation, as if a rod is prodding me right through my empty belly and all the way out. I shiver with cold. It will most probably get even colder as the sun goes down, but I still have half a day left.

The air down here is humid. My skin feels cold, almost wet to the touch. I can only hope it won't get too cold tonight. I might freeze to death. My instinct kicks in. Desire to survive overpowers the fear and I look around. My inner wolf flares up, its eyes surveying the place, adjusting to the darkness that reigns within.

It's hard to focus. All I can think about is meat and juices running down my chin as I devour it. The very thought is making my mouth water. My stomach growls loudly, angrily. It packs a vengeful punch.

My ears prick up. I can't hear anything, not even the wind blowing. I don't know how long it took me, but I eventually fall asleep, curled up on the cold floor.

When I wake up again, it's because I hear a sound. It's a loud thump noise. My nostrils immediately recognize the smell of meat. My stomach is now a gaping wound begging to be filled. I look to my right. There is a small, wrapped up bundle. That's where that heavenly scent is coming from. I swallow heavily. It's hard to remain impassive and not jump at it immediately.

I look up. The guys are back. Their heads are bent downward, looking into the hole. The prison cave. They can call it the cave of cleansing all they want, but this is what it truly is.

"You taking me out to dinner, I see?" I say, as I look at the clouds behind them darkening.

A million thoughts start swarming inside my mind, like angry bees threatening to start stinging any moment. Why would they bring me anything? Am I even supposed to touch it?

"After everything you've been through, we thought we could cut you some slack," Vlad explains. "Just, don't tell Taarus. He'd have our hides for it."

I try to focus my gaze, but my vision is blurry. The smell of meat is overwhelming. It's unbearable, beckoning me to tear apart the packaging and sink my teeth into it. Only, something urges me not to.

"Thanks," I tell them.

I'm still not in the pack, or whatever they want to call their grouping here, in this place. So, why would they want to help me? Why would they go against the rules and give me food, when their leader had strict orders against it? The wolf in me growls silently at this generosity.

"No matter what you hear, don't pay attention," I hear Stefan's voice. "There are no monsters coming for you in the dark. Only the ones you yourself have created."

I frown. "Great. The real danger is inside my head, the only place I can't run away from."

"She's funny," I hear Vlad whisper to Stefan, and he probably thinks I didn't overhear that, but the cave is so silent that every sound from up above is brought downward with the force of a horn.

"We'll come in the morning," Stefan adds, then within seconds, their heads disappear from the opening above me, and I am alone.

The clouds have gotten even darker now. I recognize that color. The sun is setting quickly. Much more quickly than I would like it to. I pray for sleep to come to me, but anguish is keeping it at bay. I have no idea how I fell asleep before, but I'm sure that I won't be so lucky this time.

I glance at the meat once again. It's tempting, but much less so now. It's tainted with suspicion. Maybe it's poisoned? Maybe this is how they deal with the unwanted newcomers? I snort at the meat, as if it were a living thing. I want it to know that I won't touch it, no matter how horrible this ache in my gut becomes.

The Hermitage has always been known as a refuge, the last place to go when there was nowhere else. Now, it turns out they have rules of their own. They don't just open their doors and welcome you in with open arms. I was silly to think it would be so. I allowed them to trap me here. Without a clan, without a father, a family, I am all alone. I am trapped inside my own life. Does it really matter if my body is physically trapped?

I close my eyes and I can see him. My father. The image I have of him in my mind's eye is still burning bright. He was a fair man, a kind man who fought for equality, a man who fought for justice. He didn't care about the repercussions of his actions, as long as he was led by higher ideals.

A part of me is angry with him. If he were any different, then I would still have him by my side. I would still be living in the pack, and although it wasn't the best kind of life, for Kaige differentiated between us all, I would still be happy because my father would be with me. Now, I have nothing. My heart is enraged and saddened at the same time, and these two emotions are difficult to reconcile. My father took responsibility for the things he's done, and this is why I am where I am.

But, at the same time, I can't but not think him a great man, a man who possessed grace and dignity, who fought for those who could not fight for themselves. That was my father. A good man, a kind man, a brave man, a man who was killed like a worthless animal.

Rage boils inside of me once more, and I feel no more hunger. The sensation inside my abdomen has completely vanished. Only rage remains. I put sorrow aside, because I can't afford to shift my focus from revenge. I don't know how yet, but I know that I will avenge my father's death.

Chapter 4
Cat

The night is restless, filled with shadows which seem to aim their dark claws at me menacingly. I know that I cried, but I couldn't even feel it. I brush my cheek with my hand and that is when I feel wet streaks running down my cheek. My misery is mine alone. Even the tears have dried up after a while. Crying will do me no good.

I am afraid. I should be afraid. Fear will keep me on my toes. It will keep me vigilant. Tears will only make me bow my head down and lose focus of the only thing that matters right now. Surviving.

Exhaustion wraps its heavy arms around me tightly. Nightmares plague me every time I close my eyes, and I don't know what's worse: opening my eyes and seeing the desolate darkness of my current condition or closing my eyes and allowing the demons of my past to catch up to me.

I put my knees to my chest. The smell around me suffocating. Mold and dirt. Suddenly, there is a noise. Some kind of chirping. My heart races with fear, but I know any animal I stumble onto while here couldn't be worse than my enemies up there. It must be the bats, I try to comfort myself. For a moment, I even manage to do it.

It's hard to remember the good old days, the peaceful days. It seems that ever since he had become the pack leader, Kaige didn't allow any of us to have a single day of peace. Our previous pack leader was strict but merciful. He was fair. We learned to rely on him to make the right decision which would benefit the entire clan, not just himself. But, it all changed when Kaige came to rule. He wanted to control every element underneath him, the people, the animals, even the nature. Of course, we all rebelled. We had to bide our time and wait for the right moment. When it seemed that the right moment came, my father acted. Only, with devastating consequences.

I still remember my father's voice as vividly as if I heard him a mere hour ago. His voice is whispering to me in the depth of this night. It is telling me to be brave, to accept my fear and let it guide me. It's hard, but I have to try and do it… for him, for myself.

Thinking about him hurts so much. I never thought anything could hurt this much. I feel like this anguish will kill me before Kaige has a chance to do so.

What do you want?

I suddenly hear my father's voice in the depth of the cave. I open my eyes, and for a moment, my heart believes he's come back, that the horrible images I saw weren't real, that it was just a distorted reality. Only, his death was real. It's as real as the darkness around me.

I don't know what I want. But, I know I don't want to die. I want to live. I want to breathe. I want to survive, and find Kaige and then… I don't care what he does to me. He might as well kill me. But, I must try and avenge my father's death. I must show him that no matter how evil and frightening he is, there will always be someone with enough courage to stand up to him.

The thought of moving on alone, without my pack makes me shiver, but not from the cold. My mind wanders all over the place, then finally I think I see the first outlines of sunlight oozing down the hold above me. The darkness becomes penetrable, and when I lift my gaze, the sky assures me that somehow, someway, things would be alright. I try to believe it.

Suddenly, I hear the sound of footsteps. Only they aren't coming from anywhere above me. I turn around. My ears prick up. I feel like I'm hearing it wrong, but I know I'm not. The sounds are coming from inside the cave, the sound of footsteps. Someone is coming.

I remain in the light, my eyes trying to pierce through the still thick veil of darkness around me. I try not to blink even, for a moment could cost me a second of reaction time, and I could be a goner. My breathing is rapid. I can almost hear my own heartbeat inside my head.

"Ecaterina," I hear my voice echo inside the cave.

"Who is that?" I shout back. I'm absolutely terrified, but I'll be damned if I'll let it show.

My eyes are peeled open. Then, three silhouettes appear. I recognize Stefan immediately. Vlad is behind him. Finally, the third man is Taarus. He is walking slowly, that same cape around his neck, dragging itself like a snake along the floor after him.

I see that same bundle they threw down to me with the corner of my eyes. I haven't touched it. I don't even smell it anymore. I wait for all three of them to come before me. A match lights up an oil lamp, and I welcome the light. Their faces are recognizable, and whether they come as friends or foes, I still welcome seeing someone. Anyone.

I watch as Taarus looks to the side, at the bundle.

"You haven't eaten," he speaks. I just shake my head. "Good."

My lower lip trembles. So, was it really a test?

"They were supposed to give it to you when you were the weakest," he explains.

"That they did," I frown at the guys, but all I see on their faces is a weird kind of gladness. What were they so glad about? "What would have happened if I ate it?"

"You would have died," Vlad jumps in. "It's poisoned, you know."

"Are you serious?" I'm shocked to hear that. "So much for your hospitality and acceptance."

"He's lying," Stefan gives him a dirty look, then elbows him gently. "Of course, it's not poisoned. Nothing would have happened to you if you ate it. I mean, nothing physically."

"What do you mean?" I wonder.

"I'll let Taarus explain," Stefan nods, giving the word over to Taarus, who hasn't taken his eyes off of me since the moment that oil lamp illuminated us all.

"We accept everyone," Taarus explains. "This test merely shows us how you react to outer stimuli."

I'd like to tell him all about the stimuli I just had, but my throat burns, and I can't get a single word out.

"What does my reaction tell you?" I truly wonder.

He takes a moment before replying. "It helps with the placement."

I'm a bit annoyed that he's talking as if I've been here for ages, and I know exactly what he means. I don't. My mind is still too focused, trying to process things that just happened, and I hoped I would be welcomed here with open arms, not forced to prove myself.

Maybe they are waiting for me to ask about the placement. I don't. Nor will I.

"The Hermitage welcomes all outcasts," Taarus continues. "But, this is a society like any other. We are a clan, only there is no leader."

"I thought you were the leader."

"Spiritually, yes," he nods. "I am here to offer guidance and any help that is necessary. But, I don't like to consider myself a leader. People are free to leave this place any time they wish. However, if they do remain to stay, there are certain rules that need to be followed."

"I don't mind rules," I reply.

"I'm glad to hear that. There is no hierarchy here. We are all the same. The food is shared equally, and so is everything we have."

"I understand."

"Also, this place functions as it does, solely because of the people who put so much effort into it. That is the placement. Seeing what your character is made of, and then assigning you to a job that would be most suitable for you."

"I can be much more than a mushroom picker, I swear," I glance over at the guys.

"Hey!" Vlad frowns, and I can see it even in the darkness, as his brow furrows. Actually, being pissed only makes him even more attractive, if such a thing is possible.

"Let's feed you properly first," Taarus doesn't reply to my comment, and Vlad also calms down. But, I'm sure he'll deliver his reply. "And then we'll see how you can best help us here."

With those words, he turns around and disappears back where he came from, leaving me with the guys.

"I'll have you know that mushroom pickers is one of the toughest jobs there is." As I thought, Vlad immediately retorts.

"I'm sure it is, Goldilocks," I snort.

"Actually, he's right," Stefan confirms, and his tone of voice allows nothing other than agreement. His steel blue eyes seem to pierce right through me, and I almost stumble backwards. "We go out of the safety of the Hermitage. We risk our lives to get those mushrooms."

"Why do you need them?" I wonder. "If it's for food, isn't it easier to just grow some close by?"

"These aren't just ordinary mushrooms," Stefan shakes his head, and a few loose curls fall over his eyes. "It is this single type of mushrooms blended together with the powder of just one petal of wolfsbane – "

"Wait, isn't wolfsbane poisonous?"

"It is," Stefan confirms again. "But, one petal won't have such an effect. It'll make you a little sick. You'll start sweating, as if you have high fever. Maybe some vomiting, too. That's different from person to person."

"OK then, if it makes you feel like shit, why would you take it in the first place?" I don't get it.

"It's only to be taken in the most dire of situations," Stefan explains. "Like when you are on the brink of dying. This will make you feel horrible, but it has the power to bring you back from the dead."

"Maybe she'll be chosen to come with us," Vlad suddenly ponders.

"I doubt it," Stefan shakes his head, giving me a once over which insults me a little, as he obviously doesn't see me fit enough to join them.

"Why?" I frown.

"No offence, but you'd never be able to keep up."

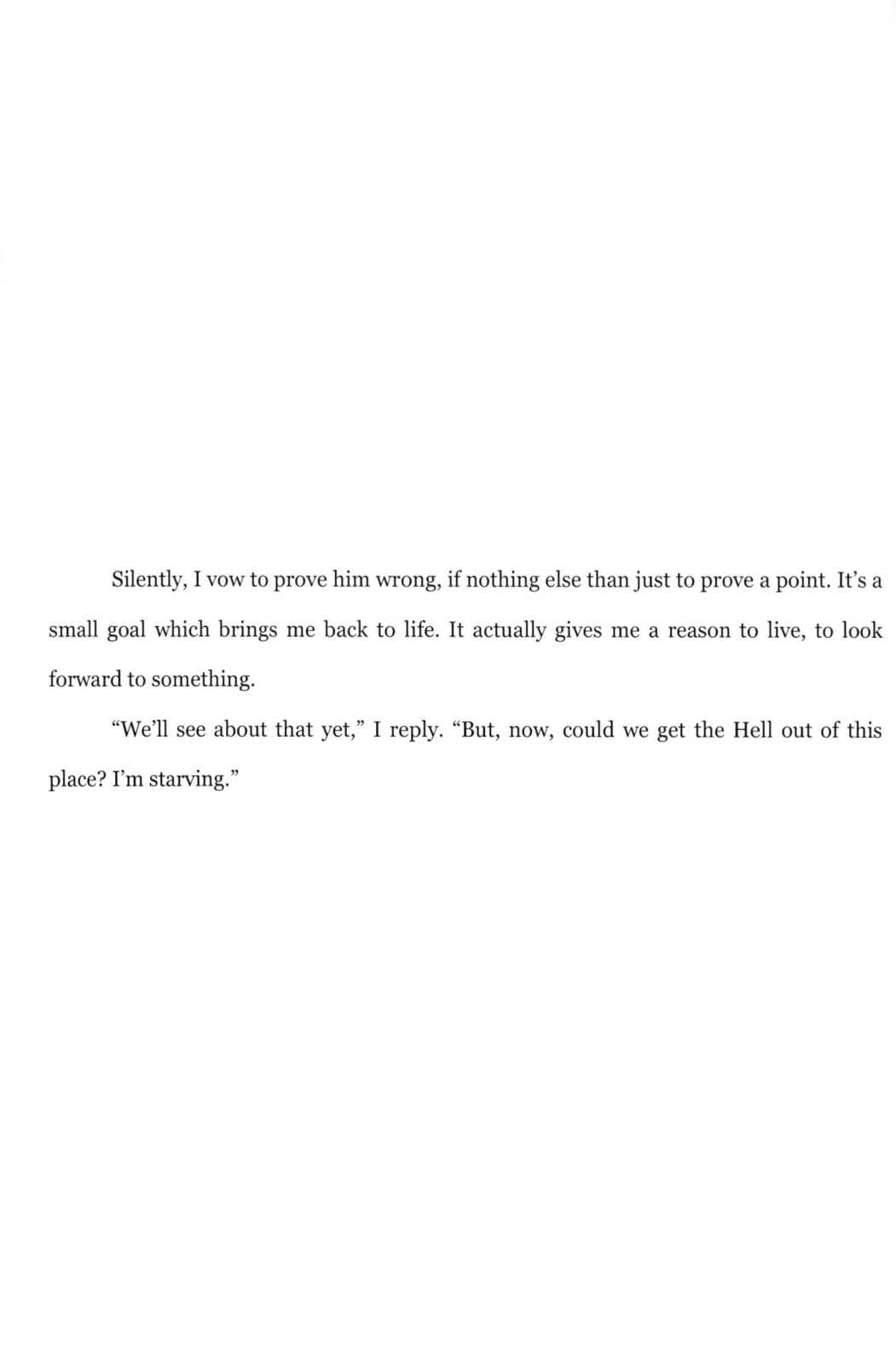

Silently, I vow to prove him wrong, if nothing else than just to prove a point. It's a small goal which brings me back to life. It actually gives me a reason to live, to look forward to something.

"We'll see about that yet," I reply. "But, now, could we get the Hell out of this place? I'm starving."

Chapter 5
Cat

The guys take me to the dining hall, which as they explain is where they all share their meals. Large windows which seem to be made right in the walls of the very mountain let in enough light. As I pass by one, I glance outside. All I see is the blueness of the skies.

The tables are ordered neatly, in three long rows. The chairs are simple, wooden, stacked close to each other, as if to symbolize the closeness of the people who occupy them. The floor is hard, made of stone. There is a constant chill about this place, but it's because we're inside the mountain itself. Of course, it's going to be chilly.

The guys lead me to the closest seat, and despite all my expectations, Stefan pulls the chair for me to sit down.

"Thank you," I say not really because I'm grateful, but mostly because my parents taught me proper manners.

At that very moment, a lady comes in carrying a tray in her hands. She walks over to us slowly, then places the tray on the table. The first thing which reaches me is a bowl of the most delicious smelling soup I've ever laid my eyes on. Or, maybe it was that I was starving. In either case, I can barely prevent my hand from quivering, as I wait for the lady to put a spoon next to the bowl.

"Thank you, Willow," Stefan smiles at the lady.

She has a kind face, one which has born witness to many hardships in life, but which still doesn't want to burden anyone with it. Instead, she has a smile. Her eyes are a dark chestnut brown, and her cheeks are slightly sun-kissed, probably from the time she spends in the sun. She places a fork, along with a knife by the bowl in front of me, and I lower my gaze to see burn marks on her hands. Curled up skin, roughness and dark spots which will probably never disappear.

I immediately look up. I'm not sure if she's seen me looking at her hands, but I don't want her to catch me staring at her. The last thing I want to do is make anyone here feel uncomfortable. So, I look away, and my eyes meet Stefan's.

"This is Willow, our cook," Stefan explains. "Willow, Ecaterina."

I raise my gaze back at Willow. Her lips have widened into a welcoming smile.

"It's very nice to meet you, Ecaterina," Willow beams at me warmly.

"Cat is fine," I smile back. "Likewise."

"I hope you like French onion and mushroom soup, Cat" she continues. "The ingredients are so fresh that they were still a part of Mother Nature mere hours ago."

"It smells divine," I assure her, and my stomach rumbles in response.

Willow chuckles. "Look at us, yapping away, while you must be starving, dear child."

"I am a bit hungry," I nod shyly, still somewhat reluctant to pick up that spoon and devour the soup in one go.

"What are you waiting for? Eat," Willow urges me, and I don't need to be told twice.

I grab the spoon and start shoveling the soup into my mouth, chewing on the juicy, tender pieces of mushroom and onion. I know they're all watching me, but I can't pay attention to manners right now. The animal in me has taken over, and it needs to feed.

As soon as I'm done, Willow takes the empty bowl and places another plate before me. This one looks even more appetizing. It's fried veal, with barbecued potatoes and little bowls of dips and sauces, all of different colors. I could open my mouth and just swallow all of it in one go. That's how hungry I am.

Slowly, I poke at the potatoes and the meat with my fork, feeling the ache in my stomach subside. When I'm done, I put the fork down, but it seems I'm still not completely done because Willow places a dessert plate before me, and if my eyes aren't fooling me, it looks like forest fruit cheesecake.

"Did you make all this?" I watch the dessert in awe, reluctant to ruin it with my fork.

"Of course," Willow sounds proud, as she should be.

"And, you alone cook for everyone?" I wonder, still unable to take my eyes off of the plate.

"I do have some help in the kitchen, but yes, I mostly do it all," she says even prouder now, with a victorious little smile on her thin lips.

"Amazing," I shake my head incredulously. "That must mean you spend all day in the kitchen."

"You could say that," she chuckles. "But, I do it because I want to."

"I'm guessing you also didn't eat the meat they threw you while in the Cave of Cleansing?" I ask.

Immediately, I turn to the guys, not sure if this topic was supposed to be a secret of some sort, or if we're all allowed to talk about the test and how we did. As soon as I mentioned the meat and the cave, she shakes her head at me.

"Actually, I ate the whole thing," she smirks. "Licked my fingers after it. You could say I failed the test."

"But, nothing happened to you," I wonder. "I got the impression we're not supposed to fail the test."

"Oh, it's some pish posh Taarus writes down in his little black notebook about us all. Apparently, it helps him learn things about us, things we aren't readily and consciously willing to share. Then, he discusses things with us, trying to figure out what our strong suits are. I've always been a cook, even though I never bore the title. I can make soup out of dirt and roots so deliciously you'd lick the spoon. Of course, he wouldn't make me a mushroom picker."

"About those mushroom pickers," I continue.

"You should ask Stefan and Vlad, they'd know," she aimed me in their direction. "But, you get the job best suited to your skills."

"What if I have no skills?"

"Everyone has that special something they do better than everyone else," she assures me. "Taarus will know. He always knows."

I smile back, then dig into the dessert. I finish it in a heartbeat. Willow seems pleased as she takes all the plates and puts them back on the tray.

"I have to get back now. Lunch will be served soon. We can't leave the people hungry."

She winks at me, then disappears as quickly as she appeared. Then, I turn to the guys.

"OK, now what?" I ask.

"You're very impatient, do you know that?" Vlad tells me with a flicker of a smile, yet there is no bitterness there.

"I just want to know what will happen to me," I explain.

"Your fate was unresolved up until the moment you reached this place," Stefan continues. "Now that you are here, there is no need to be impatient. You are where you need to be. You will know everything when the time comes."

"What do I do in the meantime?" I frown, feeling like a little child who was just scolded.

"Well, what do you want to do?" Vlad surprises me with his question.

I can't figure him out. In fact, I can't figure either of them out. They're both a mystery, and every time I glance in their direction, I feel like there's a strange new desire forming inside my very soul. I have no idea how things work here, but my gut tells me I belong here. I came exactly where I needed to come. Some higher forces brought me here, and I guess all I need to do now is learn some patience, which is easier said than done.

"I want to see this place," I say, as my curiosity takes hold of me. "I've seen where you eat. Where do you sleep? What do you do here for fun? Or, is it all work?"

"It's not all work," Vlad is quick to reply. "And, we can show you all of that, but first, we need to wait for Taarus to come."

I glance back at the door. It was still just the three of us.

"Where is he?" I ask.

"Busy," Stefan nods. "It's not an easy task handling this place on his own."

"So, he leads this place, but he isn't the leader? That still makes no sense. You can't have a clan without a leader."

"He isn't the leader," Stefan repeats. "He doesn't like to be called that."

"But, that's what he is," I frown. "You want me to call milk black just because it won't accept that it's white?"

"He hates the term, because…" Stefan starts, then his eyes fall upon the door, just to make sure that no one would barge in unexpectedly and overhear him talking. "Because, he once belonged to a clan called the Whitefangs."

"The Whitefangs?" I repeat.

Everyone knows the story of the Whitefangs. It's a story my father used to tell me before bedtime. It was supposed to teach us that family always comes before anything else, and when someone decides to stomp on family and all it stands for, then only tragedy can follow.

"He was one of them?" I ask incredulous. "I thought the clan went extinct."

"Almost," Stefan nods. "Taarus is the last one."

"So, the story of Xenos is true?"

"Actually, his name was Rasvan. As the story kept being told and retold, somehow the names got changed. Maybe those who told what happened wanted it mixed up like that, I don't know. But, I do know that Rasvan and Taarus were brothers. The only sons to the Alpha, by the name of Miron."

As he's telling the story, bits and pieces of what I know start coming to the surface. My father told it to me when I was a child, and honestly, I always thought it was one of those legends which had more falseness to it than truth, and which was created to frighten the young ones into obedience or merely just to teach them that there is evil in this world.

Whatever the purpose of the story was, it was achieved. I do believe in evil. I always have. I guess all of us half wolves, half humans do. It's like an echo of a threat that is always present, always there.

"Rasvan poisoned everyone," I show him that I know the story. "His entire family. His mother, father. Even his baby sister."

"You know the story," he lifts his eyebrow at me.

"We all do," I nod. "Rasvan also poisoned his brother, Taarus."

"Yes, his body had almost died, but his will to live was far too great. His heartbeat was down to a barely audible whisper, a forgotten echo of a beat. That's why Rasvan thought him dead. He ordered for all the bodies to be taken out and thrown onto a pile, then burned. When the guards weren't watching, Taarus managed to crawl away, every move feeling like a million needles were stuck in his body at the same time. He reached the Wailing Woods and fell unconscious by a brook. When he woke up, there was a small pile of berries and mushrooms by his side. Someone brought them over for him."

"But, who?" I wonder, always liking this part of the story, even as a small child.

It proved that even in the face of all that evil, there was always goodness in the world, when you least expected to find it.

"Taarus never told anyone who it was," Stefan shrugged. "Many think it was the spirit of the forest, materializing somehow, enraged at such an act of injustice."

"I can't believe he survived all that."

"He did. It just proves that something good can come even out of the most wicked deed. Because, if Rasvan hadn't done that, then Taarus wouldn't have come up to the Malefic Mountain and he wouldn't have established this place, which is a refuge for so many of us."

"So, he doesn't want to be considered a leader, because that is what Rasvan wanted to be," it finally hits me. "He wants to be nothing like him."

"Exactly," Stefan confirms.

I glance at Vlad, but he doesn't seem to have much desire to join this conversation, but I can see that he's listening intently.

"There is no leader in this safe house," Stefan reveals. "We owe him our loyalty and gratitude not because he is our leader, but exactly the opposite. He is our friend, our savior, our defender, and we are all the same to him."

"I guess I never saw it like that," I admit. "I thought this place was just like any other clan. Only we all gathered here out of sheer necessity, we weren't born into it."

As I gaze into his eyes, it's impossible not to believe every single word he says. I inhale deeply, and I can't escape his scent. It's wild, untamed. He smells of the woods, of moss and morning dew. He has a mindless energy which keeps drawing me towards him, although he hasn't done anything to show me that he would be even remotely interested in bonding or mating. I suppose people here don't consider it important. Mating is the last thing on your mind when you're trying to survive.

"Come," he suddenly gets up, and I know that our conversation has come to an end. "Taarus said to bring you to him once you were fed."

I may be fed, but I doubt I'm ready for any of this. But, there is nowhere else to go, nothing else to do. So, I follow, not knowing where this rabbit hole will lead me and if I will ever surface out from it.

Chapter 6

Stefan

"I can't believe I have to go with you guys," Cat says, through the usual morning sound of birds.

Vlad and I've walked this path a thousand times. We know where it leads. We know every single treacherous turn, every single nook and cranny on these trees and in this dirt. But, with her around, it seems like a new path.

"That's karma for ya," Vlad replies with a chuckle. "You made fun of mushroom pickers, so now you're one of us."

"I was hoping I'd get something to be done on the inside of the premises," she admits with a huff. "You know, something that wouldn't make me walk too long or too far away from this place."

"You scared?" Vlad asks.

"No," she spits back, a little insulted that he would even think that. "I'm just overwhelmed with everything, that's all and I expected to get some time to recover and not be pushed into what I just found out was one of the jobs with the most responsibilities."

"None of us here decides what we're going to do," I remind her. "Taarus knows, and we trust his judgment."

She doesn't listen. Or, if she is listening, there is not a single sign that she plans on replying. She suddenly stops in the middle of the path, opening her eyes to the early morning sunlight, which oozes through the branches over our heads. Vlad and I always go early in the morning. Not only because it is safer to do the picking during the daylight, but also because of visibility. It is easy to mistake a poisonous mushroom for a nonpoisonous one and put it in the wrong pile. Willow does possess some knowledge about mushrooms, but she expects us to do our jobs, just like we expect her to do hers.

I watch as she lifts her arms into the air, stretching. It's still early in the morning. Vlad suggested to leave it for the following day, because Cat needed her rest. I watch her bare legs in a pair of shorts. There are a few bruises on her knees and shins, probably the result of her traversing the entire length of the Wailing Woods to get here. Some are green, some purple, while a small part has already started to turn yellow.

She starts to hum something, and although I'm generally not a fan of humming, I can't stop listening to her or watching her. Her voice is so soft and melodious. Her appearance here has been so unexpected. Everyone who has come to the Hermitage has come broken and hopeless. She also came broken, but the fire of defiance and life still burned inside of her. She was hungry. She was angry. She was bitter. She was vengeful. None of those traits can be found inside someone who has given up on himself and on life.

I remember coming here myself. My sides bleeding. My body marred with cuts and bruises. Pain searing through me. Everywhere I looked around, I just saw haze. I was barely able to keep my eyes open. But, I managed to reach this place. Taarus opened the door and took me in. Two days later, Vlad also found this place. Remembering more than that is too painful, even after all this time.

"So, how do I even know which mushrooms we need?" she asks, as she lowers her arms back down to her thin frame, which seems easily broken, but it's not.

Her body may be frail, but I've gazed into those eyes. There is fire the likes of which I've seen only in the fiercest of warriors.

"You'll just be carrying the basket for the time being," I tell her, glancing at the basket which is now resting in her hands. "Vlad and I will do the rest. You just watch, and as we go, we'll show you differences in the mushrooms themselves which might mean the difference between life and death for someone."

"Also, we have some books you could read," Vlad jumps in, reminding me about the books which we've put aside for her to go over.

"Yes," I nod. "It's just theory, but the more theory you know, the better you will be able to put it into practice while we're out here."

Suddenly, a flock of birds explodes from a tree in the distance, scattering about in the morning sky. We all freeze in spot. My knees bend, my ears prick up, listening to any sound which might mean that we're in danger.

The Hermitage is a safe place, yes. But, the Wailing Woolds and the Malefic Mountains are still a world where animals rule. Not us. We are just guests here, and we need to tread with caution, lest we want to become food for those higher up in the food chain than us.

"What is that?" Cat asks, and I gesture at her with my hand to be quiet.

"Shhh," I hiss.

I'm still alert. Whatever frightened those birds might be on the prowl, it might be hunting. Us.

We're all listening. Vlad's eyes are focusing on something in the distance. He is trying to catch its scent. But, I doubt we're close enough. There is too much pollen in the air, too much other smells for us to pinpoint from this distance what that something could be.

"Check it out?" Vlad whispers. I just nod.

I show Cat to stay close behind. We try walking as noiselessly as possible, but it's hard. The forest floor is filled with dried twigs and branches, and it is hard to avoid every single one of them. This is much easier to do in our wolf form but shifting just to see what that noise was makes no sense.

The forest is strangely silent. Minutes ago, we could still hear the chirping of the birds and even bees in the distance. The forest is alive, especially at this hour. Now, it seems that the forest has closed up onto itself, as if in an effort to hide from some unknown threat.

I notice a few broken branches of a bush nearby. I point it out to Vlad, and he nods. Whatever it was, it passed through here. I look down, trying to catch a glimpse of some footsteps, but nothing is discernible. We keep walking in the direction of the birds. Suddenly, I notice a few drops of blood. All the hairs on my body stand on end. Blood is never a good sign. I don't even need to show it to Vlad. He's already seen it.

I turn around, just to make sure Cat is still with us. She's moving as silently as we are. She's bent slightly forward, shifting all of her weight so she moves with greater ease. Whoever taught her, did a good job.

Now that we've noticed blood, it could be only two things. Some poor creature fell prey to a bear or other similar predator, or whoever we're running from has figured out where we are and came looking. My entire being hopes it's a predator. That we could handle much more easily than an assassin sent from one of our clans. For, there are many wolf shifters at the Hermitage from different clans, and any of them could be the target. Hell, even the three of us could very well be.

Then, I see Vlad pointing to a tree right in front of us. I glance in the direction of his finger. A wounded doe is lying at the bottom of a tree. Half of her body is hidden from plain sight, as she lays her head onto a pile of dried leaves. Her breathing is quick. She's frightened, and rightfully so. The pink and red flesh of her hind leg is torn open, and the blood oozes onto the grass underneath her. Her eyes are wide, as she watches us approach, unable to move.

I come to her first. Vlad and Cat are behind me.

"Oh my gosh!" I hear Cat exclaim, pressing her hand to her lips.

As a wolf, she should have seen scenes like this before. Maybe she hasn't shifted as many times as Vlad and I have, or maybe she had someone to keep her safe from the harsh reality of life. Only now, she has to stare at it straight in the face. She can't hide from it any longer.

"What happened?" she asks, unable to take her eyes off of the doe. "Who could have done this?"

"Someone who heard us coming and just left her, the poor thing," Vlad explains.

I wonder if a bear would have run away from us. I doubt it. Another wolf also wouldn't have left its prey, especially if it were hungry. The only logical conclusion that comes to mind is that she was left for us to find, in this condition. To frighten us? To warn us? And, who exactly – Vlad and me or Cat?

"We can't leave her like this," I whisper, turning to them.

"What..." she starts, but the look in her eyes tells me that she understands exactly what needs to be done.

"We need to put her out of her misery," I explain.

"Can't we help her?" Cat asks, whimpering.

"This is the only way she can be helped," I shake my head. "Her ligaments are torn. She will bleed out in a matter of minutes, and every second she spends like this is pain. It will only get worse. The most merciful thing we can do is ease her suffering."

I watch as Vlad takes her further away, his hand at the small of her back. She doesn't say anything. She allows him to lead her away. I turn to the doe, kneeling down. She twitches. I can sense her pain. Her breathing is quick, shallow. I can almost see her life force leaving her body with every subsequent breath.

I extend my hand towards her slowly. She watches me intently, staring me down, still trying to determine whether I have come to inflict more pain upon her.

"I won't hurt you," I say, knowing that's a lie.

But, in this case, it is a lie masked as a truth. Sometimes, the world isn't black and white, as we all like to think it. Sometimes, it is dark or light grey, as black and white mix together. I wonder if she sees me as darkness or light.

I touch her nose with the tip of my fingers. Scorching hot air oozes out of her nostrils. She allows me to caress her, but that still doesn't mean she trusts me. I don't expect her to. Maybe she knows exactly what I've come to do. Maybe silence is her way of showing me that she forgives me. At least she does. I'm not sure if I can be forgiven for the other things I've done. But, being forgiven for this... it's a good start.

I put my hand on her neck, and the other on her muzzle. I smile at her. Her eyes are dark, like caverns. I wonder if she even sees me any longer, from all the pain. I don't want to do this. She doesn't deserve to die. But, if I don't do it, she will only be in more pain. Her eyes are begging me. Silent and cavernous.

"You've been a good soul," I tell her, certain of the truth of those words.

One quick twist of both hands is enough. A snap is heard, like a twig. Soft and almost unheard, but I heard it. Cat's shocked inhale assures me she's heard it, too. The doe's head falls lifelessly in my hand, and I rest if gently onto the ground. I close her eyes, feeling the softness of her long, dark eyelashes.

"Good night," I whisper for only her to hear.

I sigh, getting back up to my knees. Vlad doesn't have his hand on Cat any longer. She's standing by his side, on her own, staring at the doe at my feet. She looks incredulous, as if she's never seen death so close. But, I know she has. We all have.

"We need to keep going," I tell them choosing not to talk about what happened.

Not that there was anything to talk about. The story of the doe has ended. She died an accidental death I'm assuming, only being guilty of finding herself in the wrong place at the wrong time for whoever that predator was.

Chapter 7
Cat

It's been a long, troubling day, and I can't escape that feeling even nestled safely in the bed within the walls of the Hermitage. I gaze into the darkness, which is kept at bay by a flickering row of candles. The air inside is cool, crisp and I pull the covers all the way up to my neck, not because I'm scared, but because I'm a little chilly.

No matter how long I keep my eyes closed, sleep won't come to me. I keep remembering the doe and how Stefan needed to help it. I wonder if I were alone, would I have had the strength to do was what needed. Silence whispers to me in reply, and I know what it's saying. I've seen enough death to know that I can't be a part of it in any way.

I have no idea what time it is, but my inner clock tells me that if I haven't fallen asleep by now, I probably won't. Lying like this would only make me more nervous, more restless. I need something to distract me.

Then, I remember the library Vlad told me about. He only mentioned it in passing, but he pointed out the doors as he was walking me to my room. It isn't far away, only I'm not sure if I'll be able to find it in the darkness. If I get lost, I'll just knock on every door until someone opens and I'll apologize for the interruption. Anything is better than lying in bed, staring at the dark ceiling.

I push the covers off of me and welcome the cold air. It makes me alert, and any remnants of sleep that I had about me are now gone. I slide my bare feet into a pair of shoes and head for the door. I'm walking slowly, barely audibly. We're all sleeping in adjacent rooms, so the last thing I want to do is wake someone up. I push the door open equally slowly, waiting to see if the hinges would cringe. They do.

I press my lips together and close my eyelids so tightly together that they become two slits. I push it little by little, waiting each time to see if someone would stir from any nearby rooms. Once the door is open enough for me to squeeze through, I enter into a long hallway, which is illuminated by oil lamps on the sides of the walls.

I head down, almost excited to see what I will find in that library. My father owned a small library, boasting several classics and even children's books. He told me that he and my mother were gathering up all those books as they awaited my arrival, so those books always held a special place in my heart. Kaige knew that when he burned my father's shack to the ground, with everything in it, even his own sister's belongings. Only someone heartless can do that.

I finally reach the door with a small plaque on it. It says Library. I smile at the word, at the welcome notion it brings up inside of me. The knob is heavy, brass and cold to the touch, but that doesn't dissuade me. I open the door, and before I can take a single step in, I see that I'm not the only one present.

"Oh," a gasp escapes me. "I'm sorry, I wasn't expecting anyone here."

I watch as Taarus lowers the book he was holding in his hand and brings his gaze up at me. His tired-looking face seems bright now, as if it is the night time which allows him to be his most active self. The robe he is always wearing is falling onto the floor, and I can't see his feet. The chair he's sitting on is old and as he moves, it squeaks underneath his weight. Leather, I'm guessing.

"Neither have I," he replies, gesturing at the other chair which was unoccupied.

I hesitate for a moment, but then I realize that I can't just change my mind and go back to my room. I wouldn't leave a very good impression.

"Trouble sleeping?" he asks, as if reading my mind.

I nod. "How did you know?"

"Troubled minds have trouble sleeping," he explains mysteriously. "And, your mind seems to be very troubled."

I know what he is pointing at, but I'm still not ready to discuss my father. Who knows if I'll ever be? Such tragic events mar one's life forever, after which nothing can ever be the same.

"It seems that everyone who is here can be accused of that crime," I try to smile.

"Granted," he nods, a smile lingering on his own lips. "But, it is important to know that you are safe here."

"My body may be safe," I agree to a certain point. "But, one can never escape one's demons."

"You speak very wisely for one so very young."

"It is not the age you bear which shows how old you are," I suddenly remember my father's words and try to replicate them as closely as possible. "It is the circumstances of your life."

"Rumlar was a wise man," he recognizes my father's words, and for some reason that doesn't surprise me. "I can only assume that he has brought up a wise daughter."

I feel like something is stuck in my throat, and the tears threaten to leak down my face. I don't want to cry. It's not that I feel like these people are strangers. In a way, they are. But, at the same time, some of them might be closer to me than my own clan was, because they went through the same pain I did. Only such people can truly understand you.

Signaling that I don't wish to discuss my father any longer, I get up and walk over to the nearest bookshelf. I remind myself of the initial reason why I came here, and it wasn't to socialize. It was to get away from own self, if such a thing was even possible.

"We have the most obscure books you could ever wish to find," he tells me, watching my every move.

My back is turned to him, but I can sense the heat of his gaze upon the back of my head.

"Just tell me what you wish to read."

"I don't know myself," I answer, trailing the spine of the books with the tip of my finger, reading the titles. Some of them I recognize. The others, not so much. "I came to distract my mind."

"Then, perhaps I can offer you my book."

He gets up and walks over to me, offering me what appears to be an unbound gathering of several papers inside a hardcover folder.

"What book is it?" I wonder.

"It's the book of Thoth."

At first, it doesn't ring any bells. I frown as I watch the worn-out paper in my hands. Then, it suddenly hits me.

"But, I thought this book was just a myth," I gasp in disbelief, remembering the stories of ancient books my father used to tell me about.

They were the strangest books imaginable, and he always made sure to remind me that they were just stories. Most of those books were never even proven to really exist, so now, hearing Taarus mention one of them, and even offering it to me is beyond crazy. I don't even move to take it.

"It won't bite," he smiles.

"I don't know if I dare take it," I admit.

"Why?"

"If it really is the book of Thoth, then didn't the Egyptians believe that the gods' knowledge wasn't meant for humans to possess?" I ask, and his smile widens even more.

"That is exactly true," he agrees. "And, technically, it is not in the hands of humans. It is in the hands of shifters."

"We are a little better than humans?" I snort. "Or, worse?"

"That is up for debate," he admits. "Do you know anything else about the book?"

He pushes the book even closer to me, and I feel obliged to take it with a trembling hand, the hand of someone who doesn't deserve to hold such a piece of ancient treasure.

"It's supposed to consist of many texts on a wide range of subjects," I start staring at the book.

"Good," he nods, going back to his armchair and taking a seat, making me feel like I'm on a stage before a single member of the audience, whom I need to impress or something terrible will happen to me.

"Thoth was the god of knowledge," I continue, remembering my father's gentle, patient voice which always had an answer to the million and one question I had to ask him during his stories. "And, it is generally believed that he wrote all these texts. Some sources claim that there are exactly forty-two books which contain the whole philosophy of the Egyptians, written by Hermes, who was most probably Thoth before he was renamed. Hermes and Thoth were described in the same way and they both invented writing, so it's believed they are one and the same." I pause, but this time Taarus says nothing. He only looks at me with a satisfaction on his face. So, I continue. "The book contains two spells. One allows humans to understand animals, and the other spell would allow the reader to see the gods."

"Where was it hidden?" Taarus asks.

I frown, trying to remember all the details. The general story is fresh in my mind, but it is the details which I need to focus on to remember.

"The bottom of the Nile," I finally say, and he nods gently. "It was locked in a box, in a box, in a box. So, several boxes were placed one into the other, with serpents inside. It was there, until an Egyptian prince, I don't remember his name – "

"Neferkaptah," Taarus says his name, although it doesn't ring any bells, so I just go on.

"Yes, Neferkaptah, found it and killed the serpents, then opened the boxes and found the book. But, instead of blessings and joy, the book only brought him misery, because Thoth was furious that he stole it, so Thoth punished Neferkaptah by killing his wife and son. Seeing what he had done, Neferkaptah committed suicide, leaving clear instructions to be buried with the book somewhere secret."

"Very good," Taarus sounds pleased.

"But, if the book was buried with Neferkaptah ages ago, who found the book again?"

Taarus leans back into his chair, which squeals heavily. My fingers grip the book in my hands, unwilling to let it go, at least not before I take a look at it. I doubt an opportunity like this will present itself ever again.

"I did," Taarus tells me, staring me down with his dark eyes which seem to have stared into the void of life and kept some of it to himself.

"But, how? Where?" I have so many questions that I can barely blurt them out fast enough.

Instead of a reply, he gets up and walks over to me close enough so he can rest his hand on my shoulder.

"That is a story for another night," he says, heading for the door. "Good night."

Before I can say anything else, he closes the door behind him, and leaves me alone in the library, with a book I never even thought existed until a few minutes ago.

Still incredulous at what just happened, I walk over to the armchair which Taarus was just sitting on, and I take a seat. I put the book in my lap, inhaling the ancient smell of knowledge, wondering how many people have died for this book to find its way here, to this library, to my lap. I shudder at the thought of the invisible blood which must be splattered all over these pages.

But, that fear and unease do little to prevent me from opening the pages and diving into the knowledge never meant to be seen by a human being.

Chapter 8
Vlad

It's pretty late when I reach the dining hall, and I know I'll probably be the last one. Even better. I prefer having no one breathing down my neck while I eat or standing in front of me for that matter. I never liked forks and knives. Spoons are OK, I guess. But, the rest is just unnecessary.

I pick up a tray and place one of the remaining bowls of porridge on it, with some coffee and milk. Grumbling, I take the spoon. I could have just slurped the porridge, but I see there's someone still finishing their meal.

When I look more closely, I see it's the new girl.

I don't know about Stefan, but I still haven't made up my mind about her. She seems fine, a bit reserved. I'm not sure what Taarus is playing at, sending her off with us for mushrooms, but I know better than to question Taarus' decisions. If he says she belongs with us in the woods, then that is where she will be.

I walk over and sit down opposite her. She's barely touched her porridge. She's basically just flipping it over with her spoon, stirring over and over again with a frown on her face.

"I know it's not the most delicious breakfast in the world," I smile, gesturing at the porridge. "But, it's actually good for you. Lots of nutrients, and it'll keep you full for a surprisingly long time."

"I don't want to seem ungrateful," she presses her lips together, then pushes the bowl away from her. "I'm just not that hungry. In fact, I'm not hungry at all."

"That's guilt eating you up on the inside," I tell her. "You can't let that happen."

She raises her gaze towards mine. "How do I fight it?"

I see only now that she has eyes the color of peas. A beautiful, ripe green hue which is now focused on me. Her eyelashes are long, unusually dark, compared to her blonde hair and sun-kissed freckles. A part of me wonders what she looks like as a wolf. Is her fur chocolate colored? Sometimes, the eyes stay the same. I know that mine do change. My entire body changes, and there is little of my human form when I transform. I wonder if she is the same.

"You start by eating," I grin. "One bite at a time."

"You don't look like a philosopher," she replies, still not taking the spoon.

"What do I look like then?"

"A smartass."

I chuckle loudly. "Isn't a philosopher just a smartass who uses big, fancy words?"

A smile escapes her. She should smile more. It suits her.

"Philosophers usually aren't this amusing," she tells me.

"Have you met many?"

I like this conversation. I thought she was serious and a bit of an introvert, but it turns out she's quite amusing. And, easy on the eyes, too.

"No, I mostly meet smartasses," she admits, and we both chuckle. "So, I'm guessing you're the smartass, but what is Stefan then?"

"What do you think he is?" I ask.

"He's the brooding type. You know, the one that usually carries some deep trauma which isn't letting him enjoy life as he should."

I raise my eyebrow at her in surprise. She couldn't have been more right. The funniest thing is that I think she was just shooting, thinking it's probably a hit and miss. But, it turned out to be a bull's eye hit.

"Did I say something wrong?" she suddenly looks at me all worried. "I didn't mean anything offensive by it."

"No, no," I assure her, shaking my head, then raking my fingers through my hair. "I'm just surprised you saw right through him."

"Who's the philosopher now, huh?" she chuckles again sweetly.

Her laughter sounds like a babbling brook. I'm not the one to usually gush over such things, but she's got a most infectious laughter, and when she looks at you... you feel like all of your clothes have been striped off of you, and you're standing in front of her butt naked.

"Well, to be honest, all of us here carry some deep trauma," she admits. "So, taking that into account, plus the fact that he's always serious, makes it easy to guess something like that."

"I guess you're right," I reply, only now realizing how easy it is sometimes to read people, if only you know what to pay attention to. "Your trauma is your father's death."

"Yes," she nods, but she immediately looks away, and I can tell that she doesn't want to talk about it.

I understand. When we first came here, Stefan and I also didn't want to talk about what happened. Taarus never pushes anyone to share what they're not comfortable sharing. It's part of the acceptance package. He allows us the transition on our own terms. We get used to the place, the people, the surroundings, and as we do, we tend to feel more at ease here. Finally, we're eager to share. No one needs to push us any longer.

From what I can see, Cat hasn't reached that stage yet, but that's OK. She's only been here three days. The wounds are still fresh. I can almost imagine what her own mind is doing to her in the middle of the night. I remember not being able to sleep for weeks upon arriving here. I would roam through the dark hallways, focusing my mind on not getting lost and returning to my room. That is how I would tire my mind out. Eventually, sleep would come.

Only, dreams were as bad as waking life. I would see the faces of loved ones dying, calling out my name with their last breath. My heart would clench even now as I remember it. They say that time heals all wounds, but it is only partly so. There are some wounds that never heal. They just hurt less when you remember them.

"I wish I could tell you it hurts less as time goes by," I tell her honestly. "But, it doesn't. You just learn to accept it and you move on."

"How can I move on from my father getting killed just because he wanted a better life for his family, for his clan?" she asks me.

"That is the life we lead," I reply. "We choose not to be as civilized as the humans. We view fairness as scales that need to be even. Someone died? Yup. Someone else needs to die for karma not to be a bitch and come back for vengeance."

"So, what are you saying?"

"I'm saying that someone killed your father, and you think he died unjustly means that you have a right to avenge him. A life for a life."

"But, if my father couldn't kill him, how can I?"

I give her a once over. She doesn't seem like much of a fighter. But, it's not the muscles that determine this. It's the inside fire, the rage or whatever force is guiding us to keep going. If she feels it enough, then she is strong enough to beat whoever stands in her way.

"Maybe you could use a few lessons in how to fight," I shrug.

"Could you?" she jumps at me.

"Could I what?"

"Show me how to fight."

"Sure," I reply. "But, we need to do it outside of the Hermitage."

"Outside?" she frowns. "Why?"

"Because Taarus has strict rules about no fighting on the premises. Not even mock fighting."

"That makes no sense."

"Why not?" I wonder. "This should be a place of peace. Doesn't it make sense then that he would forbid violence?"

"Maybe," she agrees, but I sense there is a but. "But, we are all outcasts. We were all run out of the only place we called home, and for many of us, that was the difference between life and death. I was told by my own uncle that if he ever saw me again, he would slice my throat like he did my father's."

I frown. "Yikes. That's some messed up family you've got there."

"Trust me, you don't know the half of it," she shakes her head. "But, then again, us Timber Wolves have never been known as overly familial."

"Wait," I suddenly raise my eyebrow at her. "Your clan is the Timber Wolves?"

"Yeah, why?" she wonders, but I can tell that she senses my reply.

She's grabbed the spoon, and I wonder what she could do with it, even if she were given the chance for it.

"Don't tell me you are a Red Fang?" she asks boldly, staring me down.

"Yes," I nod, and we both take a noticeable step back.

Our two clans have been at war for decades. I could talk for days about the horrors their pack leader has done to us, so it is only natural that we retaliate.

"I was a Red Fang," I correct myself, not feeling any preferential belonging to them any longer, seeing they drove us out of the clan and threatened us with death should we ever return. "I'm not anymore, so you can put that spoon down. It really does look menacing."

She glances at the spoon, then realizes it looks ridiculous, so she drops it back onto the table before her. But, she's not taking her eyes off of me, just in case I decide to attack suddenly. Clever little thing.

"I've heard you are monsters," she tells me.

"I've heard the same about you, especially your pack leader Kaige whom I've seen do monstrous things to the young and the innocent even."

"Kaige is... "

"Your uncle," I conclude, remembering her story.

"I am ashamed to share the same blood with him," she spits angrily.

"Actually, that makes you the best candidate to take him down," I remind her. "You can challenge him."

"I can?" she asks, obviously forgetting that whoever shares a pack leader's blood could challenge him. All they'd need is a good enough reason, but one can always come up with that.

"Maybe not in the condition you are now, but surely with some practice. The question is would you want to?"

"You just told me about reaching a fair state of affairs," she reminded me.

"I did, but it takes a lot more than just sharing your blood with the alpha. It takes knowledge and acceptance of the fact that you might die."

"My life isn't worth living much as it is," she snorts.

I don't like hearing that someone doesn't appreciate their life, because all it makes me think of are all the people who weren't given a chance to live longer than they did, people who would have given anything for that chance.

"I wouldn't let Taarus hear me talking that way if I were you. He doesn't like despair. He says there is no room for it here. We left it at the door upon coming here."

"It's hard to leave it behind when that is all you feel."

"Trust me, we've all been there. Just, remember to take one day at a time. Just that."

She sighs, looking at me. Then, she grabs the spoon, digging into the bowl of porridge.

Maybe there is hope for her yet.

Chapter 9
   Cat

I take my empty bowl to the kitchen, hoping to see Willow. At first, I don't hear anything. The sinks are filled with dishes as if a small army had just breakfasted here. In a way, it has. I've never wondered how many people there actually are here at the moment but judging from what I see passing through the corridors and during occasional get togethers, there are a lot.

Suddenly, I hear whistling in the adjacent room. The door is ajar, so I knock, not wanting to interrupt whoever it is, but still hoping to catch a glimpse of Willow and thank her for being so kind to me the first time she saw me.

"Yes?" I hear a voice I recognize immediately. "Oh, it's you," she smiles upon seeing me. "And, you brought your dishes. Well, aren't you a doll?"

"Here," I smile back, feeling a little awkward, but at the same time overwhelmed by the positive energy this woman exudes.

"Can I get you anything else?" she wonders, picking up my bowl and spoon, then taking it to the previous room only to put it into the sink with all the other dishes.

"No, I'm fine, thank you," I shake my head.

"Then, you just came to bring me your bowl?"

"Well, no, not really," I scratch the back of my head. She lifts her gaze at me questioningly. "I actually wanted to thank you."

"Thank me? For what?" Her kind face beams at me, and it feels like the sun itself.

"For being so nice and kind when you met me."

"Oh, my sweet child, it is easy to be nice and kind to others who are nice and kind," she says, as she places a wet hand on my shoulder, but I don't mind. The touch of her hand feels calming and comforting, a sensation I feel like I haven't felt in ages. "So, I heard that old grump Taarus sent you mushroom picking."

"Yes," I nod.

"Not a job for a woman," she frowns.

"It's not so bad," I shrug, not really able to come up with a good reason why she might think it's unsuitable for a woman.

"It's too dangerous," she adds. "We are all here for a reason, and most of us are still hiding, knowing we can never go back, because it might cost us too dearly. Stefan and Vlad, now those two can handle themselves. I'm not worried about them. But, you… you are such a sweet child. What can you do to protect yourself?"

Her words remind me what Vlad offered. He suggested teaching me how to fight. Hearing Willow's opinion, now I think it an even better idea than before.

It's true. Everything and anything outside the confines of these walls could be deadly. Kaige has banished me, saying that I just need to stay away from their territory, but will I ever be far enough to be safe? With a man like Kaige, that is impossible. His territory always keeps changing, expanding. Who knows? It might even stretch all the way up to here at one point. Then what am I expected to do?

"That is something I need to work on myself," I say, then immediately try for a change of topic. "So, apart from doing your own work and obligations, do you people do anything fun here?"

"Fun?" she wonders. "You mean like parties?"

"Well, anything really," I shrug. "Anything that helps people forget their sad state of affairs and makes them feel a little less burdened about life."

"We celebrate the night of the full moon," she replies. "We light a fire, have a wonderful meal outside under the light of the moon."

"Do you howl at the moon?" I smile.

"No," her answer surprises me.

"No?" It disappoints me. "Why not?"

"Well, the Hermitage is still technically a secret place. Only those who are truly meant to find it eventually do find it. But, if we would be howling at the moon all together, I'd say finding us would be a piece of cake."

"Oh," I feel a little embarrassed. "You're absolutely right."

"Don't worry, you'll get the hang of things here," she assures me.

"So, all the people who live here now," I continue, because I feel that at this point, she is the only person I can really talk to. "They came here, and they are here to stay?"

"Indefinitely, you mean?"

"Well, yeah," I nod. "Or, do we have a certain period by which we need to leave this place?"

"It depends only on you," she explains. "Hasn't Taarus given you the usual run down of how things work here?"

"Most of it, yes, but I still have some questions."

"I swear, he's getting lazier by the year," she frowns like an angry mother. "You know, I was the first one to come here. For a very long time, it was just the two of us here, and when you live alone with someone like that, you find out a lot about them."

"Oh, I didn't know that..."

"Don't worry," she waves her hand dismissively, as if it's no big deal. "Not many people actually know that. Not that it matters, you know? I'm just saying it because I knew him when this place just opened its doors to people like you and me, and of course, to people like Taarus himself. He was much more... how do I put it, involved with the newcomers. Nowadays, he lets others take care of them. He just appears, like some benevolent ghost out of the darkness, then retires to his lair and sleeps, or reads, or whatever the heck he does nowadays."

"Well, he's a bit old, isn't he?" I wonder. "I don't mean any disrespect, just saying that maybe he doesn't feel up to it any longer. He's created this place, he's breathed life into it, and maybe now's the time for someone else to take over, someone younger, someone who's got enough strength and will power to do whatever needs to be done to keep these people safe."

"You know what?" she eyes me as if I've said something of the utmost importance. "That's actually not a bad idea. He should retire anyway. Enjoy his old age, and all that. And, speaking of retirement, I think I'll also find my replacement, and just oversee what's happening in the kitchen."

"I don't see why not," I shrug, with a smile.

"You're a sharp kid," she winks at me. "Now, you mind helping me with these dishes?"

"Sure," I nod.

"I was about to offer you a secret cupcake, but I see you don't need to be coaxed into helping someone," she chuckles.

"It's no problem, really," I assure her.

"And, that only proves that you deserve the cupcake even more, kid."

I chuckle at her words, and I grab a kitchen towel and start drying the clean dishes. Willow starts telling me funny stories about the people here, but nothing over the top or insulting. They're all rather endearing, and I can sense the closeness between all these people. I can only hope that they will accept me as one of their own after a while. But, I think that acceptance isn't just offered to someone. It needs to be earned. I need to prove myself somehow that I am a valuable member of this place. Then, I will truly become a part of it.

After we're done with the dishes, Willow comes through on her offer. She places two absolutely delicious looking cupcakes with purple glaze on the table.

"It's lavender," she says, as she sees me eyeing the glaze.

"Lavender?" I frown. "I do like the scent, but eating it?"

"Don't criticize something before you try it," she warns me good-naturedly, pushing the plate with the cupcake over to me.

"It does look tempting," I admit.

"And, it's good for you," she emphasizes. "It's made with honey, not sugar."

"Wow," I exclaim. "You really have everything here."

"When you can't be a part of the world out there any longer, then you create a small world in here, with everything you could possibly need."

"Speaking of which, you never answered my question."

"Which question, kid?"

"Whether we all stay here forever or we go back out there and try our luck."

"Oh, that," she nods, picking up her cupcake then taking a large, satisfying bite. I wait as she's done chewing. Then, she continues. "Like I said, no one is keeping you or me or any of us a prisoner here. We all came here of our own accord, so we can all leave, any time we wish."

"Oh..." For some reason, it sounds a little disappointing, although I'm not even sure why. Probably because I have no idea what I expected of this place.

"Did you expect more?" She raises her eyebrow at me, although there is no ill will there. She is just genuinely curious.

"Maybe that this place here is like your accommodation for the transition period."

"Transition to what?"

"To revenge."

"Ahaaa," she nods, as if suddenly, everything clicked in place, and it all makes sense now. "Revenge."

"Well, yes. Isn't that what we all want?"

"The only thing that matters is what you alone want."

I sigh. "You sound like Vlad now."

"A smartass?" she chuckles, and I have to join in, nodding. "He's one of the good ones. Stefan, too."

"I can talk to Vlad, but Stefan is weird."

"Weird isn't necessarily bad."

She adjusts herself in the chair, so that her elbows are now resting on the table that is separating us. She still has the apron on, which is surprisingly sparkling clean. I always expect cooks to be greasy and stained with food. Willow is different in that sense.

In fact, I can tell that Willow is different in many senses. I guess that was what drew me to her in the first place. She is a woman, the first woman I've met in this place and the first woman who's been nice to me here. When I look into her eyes, a muddy green color, I see a faint reflection of a mother that she was or perhaps could have been.

I would never ask her if she has kids or not. That question is too personal, and who knows what kind of trauma or hurt lies underneath. I do hope that we get close enough to talk about anything. Still, I'm not in search of a mother substitute. I know who my mother was, and no one could ever take her place. But, when you've almost died and your own flesh and blood murdered the last loving member of your family, you take all the new friends you can get.

I can sense Willow's tender heart in her words, in her voice. She is pale, much paler than many others here. I'm guessing it's because she spends most of the time cooking for the rest of us, inside these four walls. I look down at her hands. I see a few cuts. Probably losing focus when handling a knife. But, her upper arms reveal a few healed scars. They belong to a part of her life that I'm not privy to, and that's fine. Maybe one day, we could have that conversation.

"The last thing I want right now is weird," I admit. "I don't know what to expect every morning I wake up. So, I need the people around me to be predictable."

"That's asking too much, kid," she shrugs with a tender smile. "Especially the people you'll find here. They've all known heartache. Betrayal. Death. Deep, unsurpassable trauma. The last thing they can be is predictable."

"I guess you're right."

"But, that doesn't mean that you don't belong here, or that you should feel like you're in the wrong place."

"It felt like that when I first arrived here," I confess.

"Don't tell anyone, but that's how I felt, too."

"Seriously?"

"Well, yeah. Imagine coming here to only Taarus," she pretends to be shocked, and I can't stay serious. "I think he was as surprised to see me as I was to see him."

"Yeah," I laugh. "I can imagine."

"So, don't rush when deciding what your next step will be," she advises wisely. "Let yourself heal. After all, healing is what this place was created for. When, and only when you think you are in the right frame of mind to consider your next step, then decide."

"Alright," I nod, with a smile.

Maybe staying here and spending some time with these people really is the right thing to do. After all, what could go wrong here?

Chapter 10
    Vlad

A fighter's true nature never changes. That's what I read somewhere, and now that we've spent so much time here, I'm beginning to think it's really true. I have no reason to clench my fists at anyone, but they clench on their own. They're itching for a fight.

I guess Taarus predicted this well. Probably because I'm not the only one with that same problem. He keeps reminding us that there is no fighting on the premises. I try to obey this law, but it's hard when the itch hits. And, I can't go into the woods and try punching the trees around me. So, I found this room no one ever goes into, and I turned it into a private exercise room. I put everything away when I'm done, and no one has been any the wiser for years now.

I know as wolf shifters our main strength are our teeth. Forty-two teeth in total. Twelve incisors. Four canines. Sixteen premolars. Ten molars. Those teeth leave nothing to chance. They tear flesh. They break bone. They maim. They kill.

But, still, it's not always that we fight in our wolf form. That is why we mustn't keep our human body lacking in shape. Once, I almost died because I believed that I only needed to keep my wolf in shape and vigilant, that I would always have time to shift. I was wrong. Almost dead wrong. Now I know better.

I hit the sack with all the strength I have, and it comes swaying back at me, like a drunken sailor. I hit it again. Then again, until sweat starts dripping down my forehead and my temples.

I hear footsteps behind me, and I immediately turn around.

"Sorry, I didn't mean to interrupt," she says.

The new girl. Cat.

The name suits her. She comes unexpected. She's got that look that makes you rethink every single action you've taken so far and exchange it for something she'd approve of. At first, I didn't know what to make of her. But, then it became obvious. She's just like the rest of us... only she's not. Somehow, in some strange inexplicable way, she's not like the rest of us and that makes her such an enigma. I'm just wondering whether trying to decipher her will be more trouble than she's worth.

"You didn't interrupt," I shrug, feeling my fists unclench.

I wipe my forehead with the upper part of my hand, then I move to the side and pick up my mug of water, which rested on a small wooden bench. I take a big, thirsty gulp, then slam the empty mug back on the bench.

She is looking at me expectantly with those green eyes and those freckles which all seem to be kisses from an angel.

"Anything I can help you with?"

I see no point in beating around the bush. She obviously wants something.

"How do you do it?" she asks, eyeing my hands.

"Do what?"

"How do you fight?" she clarifies.

I shrug. "It's an inner feeling of readiness."

"What if you're weak?"

"Weakness has nothing to do with outsmarting your enemy."

"But, what if I'm about to take a beast?"

"In human form or wolf form?" I wonder if this is a hypothetical situation, or she has something specific in mind.

"In any form," she answers casually as if it doesn't matter.

"Well, your brain is wired differently in these two cases," I try to explain it to someone who might have never shifted before. "When you are a wolf, I guess it comes more naturally. You just follow your instinct. Your body reacts as if some inner guide is telling it what to do and every action is the right one. In human form... well, that's something that needs some polishing, as you can see." I show her my hands and the hanging sack before me.

She smiles. "Maybe you can teach me a thing or two." She eyes the sack. "It doesn't look very hard. Is it?"

"No," I shake my head. "Actually, it's not hard at all. All you do is punch it as hard as you can."

"Can I try?" she asks shyly, as if she's not asking to punch someone, or in this case, something.

"Sure," I reply, moving away from the sack. "Be my guest."

She walks over to it a little hesitantly, eyeing the sack. I can see her fingers extending, then curling into a fist. The punch takes me completely by surprise. I see her preparing for it, but I don't see it coming. The sack shakes violently, then resumes its place. Her muscles are tight underneath her glowing skin. It's hard not to want to touch it, just to see how it feels under your fingertips.

"Not bad," I reply when she turns to me and silently asks for my opinion. "Good force. Aim's not bad either. Maybe just work on your form a bit."

"Show me," she says more confident this time.

She is not demanding, but she is not pleading either. She reveals no fear, and I'm pretty sure if you'd ask her if she was afraid of anything, her answer would be no. That's a lie, of course. Everyone is afraid of something. Fear means you are on your toes. It's keeping you alert, aware of your surroundings. If used properly, fear is your friend.

It just seems she hasn't learned that yet. She's too young. One sniff and I can tell that she hasn't shifted yet. Something tells me she's too young to even consider getting closer to her, getting attached, but her power is so strong, I doubt she herself is aware of it.

"You must promise to use this only in the case of dire emergency," I grin, wondering what else she might want me to teach her.

"I plan on killing my uncle," she shoots her answer, determined to do this, even if it means surging into her own death. "So, I can't lie to you. I will use whatever you teach me to kill someone. Plain and simple."

Her lip curls up. She's bold, defiant. She's a rebellious little thing. That much is obvious. It would be a pleasure to try and tame her. But, then again she wouldn't be interesting like that. She'd be like most other girls here. Just going through the works, thinking they did something terribly wrong to deserve the fate of being an outcast.

She, on the other hand, wants to fight it. She won't accept it. And, you gotta admire that in anyone really, not just in a woman. A young, beautiful tempting woman who is standing right in front of me, asking me to teach her how to fight.

"Revenge, huh?"

"The best reason to stay alive," she shrugs.

You gotta admire her resolve, but we're all like that when we get here. We live on our desire for revenge instead of air. Then, when some time passes, we realize that there is more to life than just going after someone who almost ruined our lives. Because, if we're here and we're thriving, then they didn't really do their job, did they?

But, I can't say this to Cat. Not yet at least, because she's not mentally there yet. All I can do is agree and maybe help guide her in the right direction. Revenge is a good source of life fuel, but it spoils you eventually. It's good only for a little while. Then, you need to find something else to keep you going. Something positive.

"Some say that the best revenge is staying alive," I remind her.

"That's not enough," she growls at me softly and I know that anger isn't aimed at me.

She's such a young thing, and yet, she's got fury enough for several centenarians. I wonder if she will ever be able to let all that steam out.

"I understand how you feel," I nod, remembering my own days of wanting revenge. "We all felt that way when we were exiled, when we were wronged. For some of us, it changes."

"For others?" She gives me a puzzled glance underneath her dark eyelashes. Her gaze is mesmerizing. I never want to look away.

"Well, others left and never returned, so what happened to them is pretty much open to interpretation, I'd say." I steady the sack, then walk back to her. "But, let's focus on fighting now. Knowing a few basic punches might help you when you least expect it, because surprise, surprise, any kind of fighting, especially boxing here is a game of discipline."

"Discipline?" She sounds surprised. "I thought you just throw punches and whoever is the last guy standing, wins."

"Well, go ahead and try that, babe, and you'll be floored in minutes, maybe even seconds, because you didn't follow specific combos and strikes which actually make sense and provide you with a powerful attack as well as a chance to rest."

She frowns. "I'd rather you didn't call me babe."

"Why not? It suits you."

I don't mean it with any disrespect, and I think she immediately got that. It's just that she is so young, all you want to do is take her into your arms and protect her from the rest of the world. But, I doubt she'd take it as a favor. Rather, it'd be an insult for her, because she'd feel useless and powerless.

"OK, smartass," she pretends to frown, but there is a smile hiding in there. "Let's start with the first lesson."

"A jab," I tell her. "That should be the first punch you learn. It's pretty basic stuff, really. It's super versatile, working both on the offense and the defense. It'll also keep your opponent guessing what's your next move. Plus, if you want to retreat, it works wonders for that, too."

"OK," she nods. "How do I do it?"

"You start in the guard position, like this," I say as I'm showing her the position with my own body. She mirrors my stance well. "Then, you just shoot a straight line, like this."

She tries to do as I show her, but it's obvious that her punch is coming from her elbow.

"No," I shake my head. "A good try, though. Remember to generate power from your shoulders, not your elbows. That's where the strength is coming from. Your hand is relaxed through most of the move, then about a millisecond away from the impact, you tighten it into a fist, and you quickly pull back. Now, try it again."

She immediately does as she is told, and this time, does it perfectly.

"There we go!" I grin. "I'd hate to be your opponent right now."

She smiles. "Let's hope you never give me a reason to hate you."

"I sure hope not," I chuckle. "Now, let's try a right cross. It's a knockout punch. Only this time, your power doesn't only come from your shoulder but also from your hip as well. You have to pay attention, though."

"To what?" she asks faster than I can offer an explanation. She's fully immersed into it.

"Because you're overextending the arm, you are leaving most of your body vulnerable. So, if you want to use the right cross, use it for example, as a follow up to a jab."

"OK," she nods.

"This is how you stand," I continue, showing her with my body what is expected of her. "Your upper body is turned to your opponent. You pivot with your back foot, and you rotate your hips. Your arm extends, just remember to guard your chin with your other hand and recoil quickly, and resume guard position. Now, lemme see."

She follows my instructions perfectly, doing a smashing jab then right cross.

"Great," I nod. "You can even use the right cross as a counter punch when someone throws a jab."

She nods one more time quickly, then continues to listen. Within the next hour we go over the left and right hook, then the left and right uppercut, and she connects them all successfully.

"You're a natural," I say trying to keep my amazement down.

I was expecting many things, but for the new girl to be a natural boxer... that one I didn't anticipate. Also, I didn't want it to get to her head. There's nothing worse than a cocky boxer. Those always lose, even if their jabs and uppercuts rock.

"I already told you what my fuel is," she shrugs. "I just see my uncle's face every time I throw a punch. The rest just comes naturally."

I chuckle at her comment. At least she's being honest about what drives her. Whether it will change or not in the future, that's a different matter altogether.

"Could I come and practice with you a few more times?"

"We should really do it outside the Hermitage," I remind her. "You know Taarus' rules."

"You also know them, but you break them. Why can't I?"

Point taken. Neither of us should be breaking that rule, but then again, I'm guessing she's never dug her canines into raw flesh. Besides, I know Taarus would let this one slide, unless others find out about it and start doing it, too.

"Because I'm guessing you have more to lose than I do."

She doesn't ask for clarification on that one, nor do I offer it. Instead, she uses her sleeve to wipe the sweat off her forehead, then leaves without saying another word more.

Dammit. She truly is more trouble than it's worth.

Chapter 11
Cat

It's about 6 am the following morning when I find myself waiting for the guys. The mushrooms needed to be picked, as we had two sick people at the Hermitage, and Willow needed to make her renowned soup which, as I've heard, was enough to bring someone back from the dead. I didn't doubt it for a moment.

I see only Stefan approaching, exiting through the door and walking into the sunlight. He is his usual moody, serious self. At this point, I'm wondering how many times I've actually seen him smile. Not enough – that's the answer.

Then, I ask myself, why do I even want to see him smile? I've met so many other men here. Eligible and easy on the eyes. Not to mention flirty. But, none of them has attracted me in the same way as these two brothers have. It's almost impossible how they can even be related, and yet be so strikingly different from each other. Maybe that's exactly the charm of them. You get everything you need with them.

Suddenly, a thought occurs to me. I still haven't bonded with anyone. Kaige wanted to make sure I was expelled immediately upon murdering my father, so he wouldn't have to allow me to go through my first shift and God forbid, even make a connection with one of the other clan members. I remember my initial choice and how I almost bonded with that pathetic loser, Tidus. If I had done that, then I wouldn't even be able to consider such a possibility here. Then again, Kaige would need to fear me twice over.

But, no. I want to do this on my own. When I press my canines to his throat and feel his warm, dying breath on my face, I want him to know it was me and me alone who did it. No one else. Just me. The daughter of Rumlar.

"Where is Vlad?" I ask, without the usual morning greeting.

He frowns at me, as if he's about to say something else, but instead he just nods. "He won't be coming along."

"Why?"

"Taarus needs him," he explains curtly, as if it's a hassle to talk to me, let alone take me along with him. He probably thinks he'd be able to do what needs to be done alone and much faster than with me tagging along.

He heads out of the confines of the Hermitage, and I follow closely behind. He is walking ahead, constantly keeping a fast, steady pace, almost as if he's trying to prove that I can't keep up. But, I do. He's always just one single step ahead, and a few times when he turns around, he sees me there. His facial expression doesn't reveal whether he's glad to see that or not.

We walk for almost an hour in complete silence. If Vlad were here, we would have been talking the entire time. He'd crack a joke or two, tell us a funny story, or just be his usual amusing self. There is nothing amusing about Stefan, unless one enjoys silence, that is.

He stops in front of a large tree. At the bottom, I see a cluster of red mushrooms, the kind that Willow needs for potions. She only ever puts one in each batch, because too much might make you vomit... and that's the better scenario than the other one.

Nature is funny that way. You eat too much of something, and she rewards you with a stomach bug that might last you days. But, she rewards those who actually bother to learn her ways. You find out exactly how much of each item is needed and Nature rewards you with healing properties, lack of pain and an overall better physical and mental condition. Teach yourself or don't. The choice is always yours.

He bends down to pick them up, so I do the same. Again, we're doing this in silence, and I've almost gotten used to it. Most of the time, I have no idea what to say to him. I feel like he's my non-existent older brother's moody friend, and we're only together in situations that require us to be. Otherwise, we would be miles apart.

However, I do catch him glancing in my direction. When I meet his gaze, he immediately looks away, as if he's embarrassed at being caught. I want to tell him that it's OK to talk to other people, people you don't know, but I have no idea how to even start such an awkward conversation. So, it's easier just to continue in silence.

We're both carrying satchels, so we're stuffing the mushrooms inside, when suddenly I feel as if someone cut me with a knife on my lower leg. Pain shoots right through me.

"Ouch!" I shout loudly, pulling my leg closer to me, only to see two bright red bite marks. The skin around them has already reddened and become hot to the touch. "Oh, my God!" My eyes freeze at the sight.

I look away and see a snake with light-brown skin and a rattle at the end of its tail coil and hiss at me, as if it didn't just bite me and was getting ready for another attack. I try to pull back, but I can barely move. I'm frozen.

"Shhh," I hear Stefan say, standing up, his knees bent.

He's gesturing at me not to make another move. He himself is moving slowly, barely noticeably so. The snake isn't sure who to watch: him or me. It leans backward, still making that horrible rattling sound. Its tongue flickers at me angrily. I probably disturbed it in its sleep while I was picking the mushrooms. But, how do I tell it I didn't do it on purpose?

I feel my lower leg swelling. I press my hand to it and it feels scorching hot. I don't know if I'll be able to walk back to the Hermitage... if I will be able to keep myself conscious that is. Sleep threatens to wash over me, and I'm fighting it with every conscious effort I have left.

Stefan moves closer to me, and the presence of his body relaxes me. I don't know why, but I believe that he has the power to keep me safe. I hear him making the same hissing sounds, and strangely, the rattling slows down. The snake's tongue is still aimed at me, menacingly, but I see it is moving backwards, little by little.

I focus on it, sheltered by Stefan's body. The snake is really pulling away, as if he told her that we are no threat to it. Suddenly, she lowers herself down into the grass and slithers away. I feel like a huge rock has fallen off my chest, but when I glance back at my swollen leg, the burden is back.

"Will I die?" That is the first question that pops to mind.

After everything I've been through, the last thing I want to do now is die from a snake bite. It's just so... anti-climactic. I won't have it. I just won't.

He grabs my ankle with his hand, twists it, brings it closer to him, then gently puts it back down onto the grass. Throughout all of this, I'm clenching my teeth, trying not to show how much it hurts.

"You won't die," he tells me. "But, it will hurt a lot."

Great. That's exactly what I didn't want to hear, as I'm already in pain.

"Was it a venomous snake?" I ask, fearing the answer.

"Rattlesnakes are venomous, yes," he nods. "But, more than fifty percent of snake bites are dry. Meaning, they had no poison when they bit you."

"So, I have a fifty-fifty chance of surviving?" I frown, moaning with pain.

I don't like those odds. I don't like them one bit.

"I told you that you won't die," he reminds me, but I need more than just a friendly reminder. "Now, we need to disinfect the wound, but we'll have to do that when we get back."

He takes out a knife out of his pocket and brings it dangerously close to my wound.

"You aren't going to make an incision and suck out the venom, are you?"

He looks at me and actually grins. What I just said seems to have amused him greatly. I'm glad that at least one of us is having fun. I myself am dying here. Literally.

"That's stuff of urban legends," he shakes his head. "It has been proven not to work."

"Has it?" I wonder more to myself than to him, as I listen to my breathing become quick and shallow.

The pain is still bearable, although it is stronger than a minute ago.

"Yes," he nods. "I just want to remove your trouser leg." He slices my trouser leg and frees my ankle. "Because it will get swollen, and the tight clothes might restrict the blood flow."

I listen to his words, and somehow, I'm soothed. He sounds like he knows exactly what he's talking about. Right now, I'm grateful for such small acts of kindness. He gets up and starts looking around. Moments later, his face illuminates as if he's found exactly what he has been looking for. He rushes over and return shortly with a long, sturdy stick.

"Is that supposed to help me walk back?"

"No," he sits back down and places the stick right by my leg. "We need to get your leg immobilized, until we get you back to the Hermitage."

"But we've walked at least an hour, and that was on healthy feet," I exclaim desperately, feeling my own heartrate hasten. "I can't walk that far."

Suddenly, he presses his hand to my chest. I slap it away.

"Hey!" I frown.

My cheeks flush. Was he just trying to feel me up? I feel like punching him in the face, but I resist the urge.

"I just wanted to see what your heart rate was," he explains.

"Oh," I say apologetically, grateful that I didn't give in to my first instinct and knock him out. "Still, you could have felt my hand, you know."

I offer him the bottom part of my palm.

"This would be the most precise measuring under the circumstances."

I sigh. "OK."

I straighten my back, even arching it a little in his direction. This time, he hesitates to put his hands on me. It's almost funny. He did it without any trouble the first time, but now, he hesitates, as if we've got time to spare.

"You need to stay as relaxed as possible," he says before pressing his open palm to my heart. I feel him trembling. "Because the spread of any venom depends on your heart rate. The higher it is, the faster the venom will spread and reach your bloodstream. We want to prevent that from happening. So, you need to take deep breaths, not quick shallow ones like you're doing now."

"OK," I nod, trying to do exactly as he has instructed.

I take a deep breath, but it's hard. Breathing in deeply makes my insides hurt, and I fear the spread has already started. That alone makes me apprehensive, so my heart rate skyrockets. Then, I do it all over again. Calming down when you're freaking out is the hardest thing to do, especially when someone's telling you that your life might depend on you calming down.

Easier said than done.

"We need to limit your movement," he adds, but it sounds like he's thinking out loud and not really talking to anyone.

"We can't just wait for someone to find us here," I remind him.

"Yes, we can't," he agrees. "So, we need to get back. You'll lean against me, and we'll walk slowly."

"Well, not like I can run a marathon right now," I snicker.

Stefan doesn't even smile. I can't help but think that Vlad would find it funny. He would find a way of making this situation less scary by adding humor to it, because what else can you do?

"Come on," he says, picking me up gently, and placing my arm around his neck.

His other arm slides around my waist, and I feel his strength keeping me up. I am throbbingly aware of his arm around my waist.

"Is this alright?" he asks. All I can do is nod.

Slowly, we head back, and Stefan is incredibly attentive to the way I react. Every time he hears me hiss or groan, he stops, then asks how I'm feeling. He keeps explaining things that need to happen and things that won't happen, like me dying, which at this point, I appreciate more and more. Perhaps Vlad would have found a way of alleviating this situation with humor, but Stefan has managed to make me feel safe and protected, and like I really wasn't going to die.

He will get me back, safe and sound.

This echoes in my mind over and over again, and there is no room for doubt, not even when I feel like I can't walk any longer. He keeps me going. My entire body weight is leaned onto him. There is no more doubt in my mind that we will reach the Hermitage in time.

After about half an hour, I stop, breathing heavily.

"I can't go on..." I manage to muster. "Just leave me here and go get help. I can't take another step."

He listens to me but doesn't say anything. My arm slides down his neck, and just when I think I'm about to slump down into the grass which right about now seems like the most comfortable bed, I feel his hands around my body, lifting me up. He's carrying me like a bride, over the threshold, through the trees and the bushes which reach out to me with the thin branches, as if they're saying that I need to stay with them.

I don't want to stay here. I want to go back where Stefan is taking me.

My head nods to his chest. He feels like he is made of stone. I'm like a feather in his arms, and I hope he won't let me fly away, far away from him and Vlad. His hands are keeping me bound. I use the last morsels of energy to grab onto him.

Don't let me go...

My mind is a haze at this point, and I'm too sleepy to stay awake. I remember my father, the games we used to play. I remember his warm, affectionate smile, the way he would kiss my forehead every evening before bedtime and tell me that there is a path for everyone. Sometimes, that path may not make much sense, but that is because where we are, we still don't see the end. Once we catch a glimpse of the destination, we can truly understand the journey.

The journey I am on seems vague and bewildering right now. It makes no sense. The destination is so far away that I can't even hint at it, let alone see it. So, I stop trying.

I stop trying and allow the dream to wash over me, closing my eyes and welcoming the darkness.

Chapter 12
Cat

When I wake up, I realize I'm in a bed. My own bed, in my own room at the Hermitage. My gaze is still a bit foggy, and so is the entire room. The light which is coming from the window is mild, and I start seeing proper shapes after a few moments.

When I look to the side, I see Willow. The calm seas of her eyes are falling on me, drinking me in as if she's seeing me for the first time.

"Well, hello there, sleeping beauty," she beams at me, taking me by the hand. Hers feels soft and warm, unlike mine, cold and clammy. "You gave us quite a scare there."

I try to prop myself on the pillow, but I feel too weak.

"Wait, let me help you," she quickly jumps up, and helps me lift my head. "There."

"Thanks," I finally speak, feeling parched. "Could I get some water?"

Willow reaches for a small glass with a straw by the bedside and offers it to me. I drink thirstily.

"Thanks," I repeat. "Did I almost die?"

"Not if I could help it, kid, and as you can see, I could," she says importantly.

"Stefan promised me I wouldn't," I remember.

"Well, if he hadn't brought you here as quickly as he had, it would have been a close call," she admits.

I don't like the sound of that. Once again, so close to death. Did everyone want me dead, even nature? It doesn't seem fair.

Then, I remember. Not everyone wants me dead. There is someone who wants me alive. There are people who want me alive, people who have done all they could to save me.

"Where is he?" I ask.

"I'll go get him immediately," she gets up, but I pull her hand. She gives me a quizzical look.

"He saved me," I say, though I'm not sure if it's a question or a statement. It doesn't really matter. All that matters is that I am here, thanks to him and this woman who has somehow become my second mother.

"He did," she smiles, but then continues very gravely. "I told Taarus that mushroom picking isn't for a girl like you."

"But, why?" I wonder. "I mean, this could happen to anyone."

"I don't mean that you are incapable of doing this, I'm just worried about you," she admits. "How about I tell Taarus to assign you to the kitchen duty with me?"

I smile. "While I would love that, Willow, I really would, I still think Taarus knows what he is doing."

"You, too, huh?" she knits her eyebrows at me. "Oh, alright then." She gets up this time and lets go of my hand. "I'll tell Stefan and Vlad that you've woken up. They've been asking about you for the last several hours."

"How long have I been out?"

"More than half the day, kid."

"What about the wound?"

I pull the covers off to check it out. I notice it's been wrapped up. I try to move it, but it's still slightly painful.

"Don't move it," she advises me. "I disinfected and dressed the wound, putting some special ointment on it. You were lucky that there was only a little bit of venom inside. That snake must have bitten some poor creature just hours before it got to you, so it didn't have much venom left. That's what I call a silver lining."

I chuckle. "If you say so."

"I do say so, kid," she smiles, cupping my right cheek with her hand in a tender caress. "Don't strain too much. You need to rest, OK?"

"OK," I nod.

"I'll go and send the guys in," she smiles, then leaves the room.

I wait in anticipation the likes of which I've never known before. I'm tempted to look at myself in a non-existent mirror, just to make sure I look alright. It's OK. I've got that just-gotten-freshly-bitten-by-a-snake look. I mean, they've gotta love it, right?

Before I can think about it any further, the door opens, and I see the guys. Stefan walks in first, and Vlad barges in after him, with a small bouquet of wildflowers in his hand.

They approach me, and I try to sit up in the bed, but moving my leg still feels too painful. The discomfort is evident on my face, and Vlad immediately comments.

"Oh, hey, don't get up on our account," he winks at me.

"I wouldn't get up even if you were the freakin' king," I reply, eyeing the flowers. "Is there some other patient you're going to see after me?"

"Smartass," he grins. "These are for you."

I accept the bouquet and the moment it reaches my hands, a soft fragrance of forest flowers fills the air around me. I inhale deeply, savoring the smell.

"They're lovely," I smile. "Thank you."

"You know, you'd never think it, but Stefan actually went with me to pick them," I notice Vlad elbow his brother playfully.

Stefan seems to feel a little awkward. He obviously values his serious persona greatly and doesn't want anyone to see past it. Only, I can already see a few cracks which are tempting me to take a glance at what's happening behind his closed doors, between the walls of his mind and heart which no one other than Vlad is privy to.

"I don't think anyone can imagine Stefan picking flowers," I smile, but Stefan is purposefully avoiding my gaze. "Vlad, you should have taken a photo."

"Yeah, right?" Vlad chuckles.

"Are you done?" Stefan frowns a little, but I can see that he's not really annoyed.

He's merely pretending to be bothered by this, not wanting to show his softer side. I wonder why. There is still so much I don't know, not only about this place, but about these two as well. I feel like there is a secret I must unearth, and as each day passes, I feel like I'm a little bit closer. But, it's hard when Stefan keeps building his walls up to keep people away. I can only hope that I'm not just people to him.

"How are you feeling?" he finally turns to me.

His steel blue eyes are inspecting my face, waiting for my reply.

"Much better, thanks to you," I smile.

"I'm happy to hear that."

It feels like he's not used to having people thank him, or perhaps the feeling of indebtedness doesn't suit him. Whatever the reason, I watch him as he rakes his fingers through his curls, his muscles peeking from his short-sleeved t-shirt.

"No, seriously, I... I'm really grateful for what you've done," I change my tone to something more serious, so he knows I really appreciate his effort.

"We're all a family here," he smiles, and it feels like the sun exploded in this small room. "You would have done the same thing for me."

"Of course," I nod, absolutely sure that he's telling the truth. "But, you know, I don't remember anything after a certain point. You picked me up back in the woods and everything went dark."

"Yes, you lost consciousness," he confirms with a slight nod of the head.

He's still standing, while Vlad has already gotten comfortable on the bed, his hand resting close to my hurt leg. The physical presence has made me forget all about the pain and the itch. As I watch both of them, I realize that they actually look more alike than I initially thought. Those eyes are absolutely the same, you could never mistake them. And, now hearing them speak, there is the same soft quality to both their voices.

"I carried you back," Stefan continues. "Fortunately, I found Vlad on the doorway, as he was about to rush after us and join the picking. He knew exactly what happened as soon as he saw your leg."

"Yeah, it was like a big red chunk of meat," Vlad pretends to be disgusted, scrunching up his face and nose, as if he's smelled something offensive.

"Hey!" I chuckle. "That's my leg you're talking about."

"And, it's usually a very nice leg, don't get me wrong," Vlad replies mischievously. "But, you should have seen how swollen it was."

"So, what happened then?" I roll my eyes playfully at him, then turn to Stefan.

"We took you to Willow," Stefan explains. "She brought the ointment and the potion."

"Slathering you was the easy part," Vlad jumps in again, but neither me nor Stefan mind. He makes the story pop and we're all amused by it. "But, making you drink the potion while you were unconscious was the tricky part."

"What did you do?" I wonder.

"Willow said we need to wake you up, so I volunteered to slap you around a bit," Vlad says smirking. "It was the least I could do, really."

"Are you serious?" I gasp, but I know he's just saying it to get a rise out of me.

"You forget that half of everything Vlad says is a joke and it shouldn't be taken seriously, even if your life depends on it," Stefan suddenly interferes.

The look on Vlad's face is absolutely priceless, as he wasn't expecting such a retort, especially not from his usually silent brother. It takes all three of us only a moment then we all burst out into roaring laughter.

"Well, that was unexpected," I say once the onslaught of laughter has died down, but I'm still pressing on my sides tender from all that strain.

"It's always those silent ones who surprise you the most, isn't it?" Vlad winks at me, but I'm not even looking at him.

Stefan and I have locked gazes, and there couldn't be more truth to what Vlad just said.

"So, how did you make me drink that potion?" I wonder, reluctantly breaking the trance.

"We managed to wake you up just long enough for you to take it down," Stefan explains. "You know Willow. She can bring back the dead with her knowledge and concoctions."

"She told me that she was the first one to arrive here," I remember. "I never knew that."

"Well, someone had to be the first," Vlad shrugs. "Taarus might have created this place, but she helped mold it into what it is now. Every child needs both a mother and a father, and this place was no different than a growing child back in the day. It needed the right kind of guidance."

"That makes a lot of sense," I nod. "Well, whatever the two of them did together, it sure worked."

"It sure did," Vlad nods. "Otherwise, we never would have met you."

"Or, anyone else here," I add, for some reason feeling a little uncomfortable that he has singled me out.

The conversation picks up and we go back to usual topics, with Vlad taking the lead, for which both me and Stefan are grateful, as it's most required of us to listen. I just dive in and pay attention to the quality of Vlad's voice, which is always soothing, regardless of what exactly he's talking about. He's just a whole bag of contradictions, and you never know what to expect with him. I guess that's what makes him so appealing.

Right now, I'm a mess of emotions, and I have no idea how to accommodate this growing fondness I feel for these two guys. Especially now that I literally owe my life to one of them. Staying away from them is impossible, even if I wanted to.

So, I guess all I could do is just follow my heart and see where it leads me.

Chapter 13
   Cat

A whole week passes before I can stand on my feet properly. I have to admit, Willow's ointment has really done wonders. The swelling went down the following day already, and the pain slowly subsided as the days passed by. After about four days I was given the OK to go for a little walk around my room, the day after I was even able to go outside and feel the sun on my face. On the eighth day, I was as good as new.

I wondered how I could thank Willow for everything she's done. I know, I know. We're all a family here, and looking out for each other is a given, but I feel like she has become so much more to me, and I want to show her my gratitude in some special way.

Stefan, however, is a whole different story. Both he and Vlad came to see me every day, staying with me for a whole hour, after which they usually needed to go and do some work. They went mushroom picking four times already. It seems that we need supplies even more than usual these days.

The flowers they have brought me are still surprisingly vibrant. It must be the special powder Willow has put in the water. When I asked her what that was, she just pinched my nose in that way so characteristic of her and told me it's just a little pick-me-up for plants.

I suddenly realize that's it. I'll get her a bouquet of flowers. It might not be much, but when one's living in the mountains, surrounded by nothing but deep woods, flowers are the best way to show any kind of emotion. Just like the guys brought me flowers.

I wonder what they were trying to say with them. Glad you're not dead?

I can already imagine Vlad writing something like that on a card and gifting it to me. It'd be exactly the quirky thing you'd expect him to do. Stefan, on the other hand, isn't the kind who'd give wildflowers, unless it's the only thing available, as it is. Roses. Maybe even orchids. But, I haven't seen any such exotic flowers here. Only…

    I swallow heavily at the thought. I know where there are beautifully exotic flowers. Flowers that would make Willow's jaw drop to the floor. The only flowers that would be able to express my gratitude for what she has done for me ever since my first day here.

    I shudder at the thought of doing this. Maybe you shouldn't. I hear the rational part of my mind warning me. It's not a good idea. Well, I do know it's not a good idea. But, it's the only thing I can do. And, I will damn well do it. Even if that means going to the edge of the Wailing Woods to pick those flowers.

    I put on the most comfortable shoes I've been given, and I put two bottles of water into my backpack. Now, all I have to do is pass through the gates unnoticed by anyone. Taarus has already told us that we would be going mushroom picking the following day, which meant that all of us were free to be of use to the Hermitage in some other way.

    I sneak out of my room and tiptoe down the hallway. Every few steps I stop to listen to the possible sound of oncoming footsteps, but so far so good. I exit the home. The big yard is busy, as usual. I just need to keep my head down and not make any eye contact, so I won't need to stop and chat, and potentially explain what I'm about to do.

    I zigzag through the busy people, grateful that they're all focused on their work and not on me. Finally, I reach the door that would let me out. But, before I'm able to lift the big latch which keeps the doors closed at all times, I feel someone's hand on my shoulder.

I quickly turn around, trying to calm my breathing and not feel like a thief in the night. But, seeing Stefan only makes me feel worse.

"Cat," he says my name like it's some well ripened wine, and even I want to taste it. "Heading somewhere?"

"I, uhm…" I start but no quick and convincing lie comes to mind immediately.

"How is your leg?" he asks another question, not waiting for me to reply.

"Oh, much better, thanks," I look down at my fully healed leg that is about to take me far away from this place, and then back again. "That's why I was thinking of taking a nice stroll and enjoy some fresh air. Being cooped up in that room has really kicked up my claustrophobia."

"You're claustrophobic?" he asks gravely.

"No, no," I shake my head. "It was just a joke."

"Oh…" he says a little apologetically, and I feel bad for babbling so much. I should have ended the lie with the stroll. "Just make sure not to stray too far away."

"I will," I nod agreeably, refusing to look him in the eye, hoping that he won't notice. Only, I doubt he won't. Stefan never misses anything. I just need to lose him quickly. "Well, I guess I should be off then. I'll be back shortly, so no need to worry."

He is staring at me so intently that I can feel the heat of his gaze burning up my cheeks. Finally, I lift my eyes to meet his. I wouldn't be able to read his facial expression even if my life depended on it. A few moments pass and he doesn't say anything. Then, he smiles, and once again, I feel like the sun has come down from the skies only to shine at me. He should really smile more often. I don't say that, of course, but I think it so hard that he might actually hear me thinking it.

"Enjoy," he says. "And, don't stray too far away."

"Of course not," I smile back much less nervously, then I push the door open.

A moment later, and the Hermitage is behind me, with both Stefan and Vlad. I head immediately in the direction of the Wailing Woods, wondering if I'm going crazy or something. If Kaige finds out I'm roaming in there, even on the outskirts, he could end my life just like that, without any explanation to anyone. Maybe I'm risking too much for just a small bunch of flowers. Willow would know that I'm grateful and appreciative of what she's done even without the flowers, no?

No.

That's the only word I hear. No. Then, again and again, my mind keeps repeating it. I need to do something special. If I'm careful, no one will even know I was there. I won't even spend too much time there. Fifteen minutes, just to pick the most beautiful, most fragrant flowers, then I'll be on my way back.

Nothing will happen.

No one will get hurt.

I keep assuring myself of this as I delve deeper and deeper into the forbidden land, further and further away from the only safety I've known lately.

About two hours later, one whole bottle of water and stopping twice to put the ointment on my leg just in case, I have finally reached my destination. It is a blossoming field of the most exotic flowers I have ever seen, each more beautiful than the next, with their red and oranges, deep purples and bright pinks. The sight is absolutely breathtaking, and I know the bouquet will be as well.

Immediately, I set out to pick only the most beautiful specimens, tying them up into a large bouquet. I don't know how much time it takes me, but once I'm done, I lift my gaze. I realize, shuddering unpleasantly, that I can't hear the birds any longer. On my way here, their song followed me throughout the entire route, but now, no matter how hard I try, I can't hear a single chirp.

I swallow heavily, listening to the sound of my own breathing. I turn around. I see nothing. As far as the eye can see, it's just me and the woods. I take a step back, then another one. Before I know it, I'm running back the way I came from, and even though there is slight pain in my leg still, I can barely feel it. All I'm focused on is running and getting back to safety.

My ears are pricked up, and I'm trying to hear if there is anyone behind me, but my own feet are crumpling branches and dried leaves underneath my feet. I dare not turn around, because that might turn my fear into reality, if there is really someone behind me. So, I keep running and running until I can't catch my breath, until everything hurts so much that I've passed into the point of numbness.

I have no idea how long I've been running, but I haven't felt any cold claw on my shoulder, or any growl that might signal it's time to stop and defend myself. When I finally leave the premises of the Wailing Woods, I can see the mountains. I just need to climb up the goat path and I'll be right before the entrance. Just a little longer, I keep reminding myself, not knowing whether there really was someone after me or it was all in my mind.

The woods can have such an effect on anyone. They can make you see things that aren't there, fear things which aren't to be feared. The Wailing Woods have always been my home, but now they are exactly the opposite. If I'm not careful, they will be my burial ground.

Breathing heavily, I reach the entrance to the Hermitage. I bend forward, resting my hands on my knees, when something right underneath me makes me suffocate a scream.

I jump backward, pressing my hand to my lips.

I can't look away from the dead raven, who's had its beak viciously torn away from its face, leaving a gaping hole. I look around, but the beak is nowhere to be seen.

I wonder who would do this to a poor, defenseless animal, because the raven sure didn't tear off its own beak, nor would another animal do this. For a moment or two, I'm not really sure what to do. I can't force myself to step over the dead bird and just walk into the Hermitage as if nothing happened. I also can't stay here, just staring at it.

So, I do the only thing that feels right. I reach for the bird and pick it up in my arms. The blood has long stopped flowing from the gaping hole. Its limp body adjusts itself in my arms. I feel the softness of its wings, the utter blackness of its color.

"Who did this to you, you poor thing?" Sorrow escapes from me, as I lament this poor soul's demise.

But, the raven is silent, now and forever more. With its lifeless body in my arms, I push the door to the Hermitage open and we walk in together. I want to give it a proper burial, but I suppose I need to ask Taarus for permission first. So, I head to his study.

As I pass, I notice the strange glances I'm getting. Maybe this dead raven is speaking, only it is a language I still don't understand.

Chapter 14
Stefan

I saw her take the raven into her hands. In all honesty, I wasn't expecting her to do it. Most women tend to react differently to maimed dead birds and animals, but it appears that Cat's mind works in different ways. I watched her as she spoke to the raven, then cradled it in her arms, and walked back into the Hermitage together with it.

I counted exactly fifteen minutes. That should be enough. I still believe that she has no knowledge about me following her, except maybe for that one time when I stepped on that squirrel and all the animals within the radius of five miles dispersed, hiding away and not making a sound.

Then, she started running back. Even with that foot, she still runs like the wind. I had to keep up, although I was pretty certain that she was headed back to the Hermitage. But, what if she weren't? What if she changed directions somewhere along the way, and I lost her in the Wailing Woods of all places? I can't even imagine that happening.

So, I kept running, all the way to the entrance, when she noticed the raven. It wasn't there when she started. I know it wasn't there, because I started less than a minute after her. Someone must have put it there for her to find. But, why?

Realizing that I need to speak to Vlad about this, I push the door open, scanning the area with the corner of my eye just to make sure that Cat is nowhere in sight. She isn't, so I head inside the mountain. I find Vlad in his room, fixing the water pump.

"Oh, hey," he greets me upon seeing me.

"Have you seen Cat?"

"I think I saw her pass by and head to Taarus'. Why?" He puts down the water pump and furrows his brows. "Is everything OK?"

"Did you see what she was carrying?" I ask, watching his jaw muscles tense with every subsequent question.

"No," he shakes his head at me.

"A dead raven with its beak torn off," I whisper.

Most of us here know what that means. I'm still wondering if Cat does. Perhaps not. That must be why she was headed to see Taarus.

"Are you serious?" Vlad gets up from his chair and walks over to the window.

He rakes his fingers through his hair nervously, as he always does when he has no idea what to do with his hands. For someone usually very handy, it seems that apprehension makes him feel useless.

"Do you think I would be joking with something like that?" I frown.

"I know, I know, sorry," he immediately adds, but I don't hold it against him. I know he's as befuddled as I am.

"Someone is sending her a death message," I'm thinking out loud and Vlad is only here as a mirror to my thoughts. Although he always offers good arguments.

"But, with the beak, it's even worse," he reminds me.

"It is," I nod gravely. "A secret will be released into the world and whoever says it, will be dead."

"Do you think it's her?"

"I don't see who else it could have been meant for."

"Any of us could have gone outside," he pinpoints.

"True," I agree. "But, we didn't. I followed her, while you stayed in here. Whoever sent that message prepared this too hard to have it found by the wrong person."

"So, what kind of a secret could she know?" Vlad frowns.

"Remember that we know very little about her."

"Taarus knew her father."

"A father is one, a daughter another," I say. "But, I can't see her working against this place."

"You are a good judge of character," he replies. "Much better than I am. If you say she's OK, then she must be."

"But, what about the raven? Whose death is it predicting?"

"Maybe knowing the exact individual isn't important," Vlad comes up with one of his best theories yet. "All we know is that it is someone from the Hermitage, and that is more than enough. We need to tell Taarus, unless she's already there with him by now, showing him the dead bird."

I sigh. "I haven't seen one of those in ages."

"What I'm wondering is how someone who wasn't supposed to find us here, found us?" His question may not have been put all that correctly, but it was a crucial question nonetheless.

What many shifters here don't know is that there is a special kind of magic keeping this place safe. Taarus and Willow know it, of course, because they are the one keeping it up. Shortly after we arrived here, Vlad and I also discovered it, by accident. I doubt that either Taarus or Willow wished to share it with us, but once we found out on our own, there was no use in keeping it a secret.

The world of shifters is a world of magic, only much of it has been long forgotten. Greed and viciousness have taken over most of the clan leaders, and the bearers of magic who came from the realm of Nature decided to take it away from us, leaving just a little of it in the hands of those they deemed worthy.

I still remember the stories we were told as mere pups. There are generally four types of magic. The first one is light magic. It is the magic that Taarus and Willow were left with, to keep this place safe. It is a magic which provides strength and protection to those we care about. It is the magic of a warrior who wishes to protect. It is the magic of a mother who loves. Light magic comes from the heart. It is the heart.

Opposed to the light magic, there is the dark magic. It is the magic of loss, pain, heartache and evil. It doesn't bring protection. On the contrary, it thrives on draining life, taking one's life energy. Some also refer to it as sorcery. I've personally never seen it at work. But, it is considered lost, like the others.

The third kind of magic is the magic of renewal, the magic of Nature, the only kind of magic the human world has left. Barren landscapes explode with grass sprouts, water divides even the tallest mountain, life arises out of death. It's a constant cycle that should prove to humans that magic is still present, only they aren't looking where they are supposed to be.

Sometimes, I think that us shifters can be accused of the same sin, never knowing where to look, what to cherish, what to appreciate.

The fourth kind of magic is the magic of the world. The old magic. The magic that came from creatures far more powerful than us. The magic that can be found in the book of Thoth, the one Taarus keeps hidden in the library, safe from falling into the wrong hands.

"Is it possible that the light magic is wearing off?" Vlad ponders.

It is a perfectly valid question, one that needs to be asked to the right person. And, that person isn't me.

"We need to talk to Taarus," I simply reply. "Maybe he'll know what's happening."

"You didn't tell me where she went," suddenly Vlad changed the topic.

"Cat?" I ask, as if I don't know.

Talking about her is hard, even with Vlad, and I think he senses it. Perhaps we both sense the possibility of her being the one. I don't even know when that feeling started. I refuse to be overpowered by emotion. Such things hold no value. They only cause pain in the long run.

Instead, I focus on what really matters. She comes from a good pack. She is brave. She is relentless. She disobeys orders, meaning she follows her own inner logic, instead of blindly following orders. All of those make her a risky, albeit a high quality potential for a mate.

"Yes," he nods. "What did she want?"

"A bouquet," I reply feeling a little ridiculous.

He frowns. "A bouquet?"

"She went to pick the primrose blooms."

He whistles. "Those are nice. We should have picked those for her, too."

"We can't take that risk, you know that."

He sighs heavily. I know what that means.

"Sometimes, this place feels more like a prison than a shelter."

I understand where he is coming from. However, no one is forcing us to stay here. Taarus is always making that perfectly clear on every meeting. We are all free to leave on our own accord, and once we leave, our potential death is the result of our hands alone.

"She liked the flowers," I say stupidly. But, the look on his face tells me it's exactly what he needs to hear.

"So, what do we do?"

"The same thing we've done so far," I accentuate. "We keep our eyes on her. We keep her safe. We help her heal. Then…"

"Then what?" He turns to me, his gaze distant and a deep crease mars his forehead.

"Then, we take her as our mate."

I finally say it out loud, although we've never discussed it even once. The look on his face tells me that he has pondered that idea before but refused to share it.

"Do you think she would agree to it?" he asks.

"If you think I will play some outdated wooing game with her, then you are mistaken," I reply calmly. "I've already gone down that path and refuse to do it again."

"She's not Xena," he reminds me, as if I don't already know that.

"No one will ever be," I nod. "Because Xena is dead and Cat is very much alive. But, that changes nothing about what I just said."

"Well, you can't just expect her to say, oh, yeah, great, guys, I accept, come on!" Vlad frowns. "She's not your logical type to see everything through a set of mathematical equations."

"What is she then?" I challenge his way of perceiving her.

"She sees things," he starts much more profoundly than I expect him to. "Like, really sees them. Have you heard her talk? She speaks as if everything is a miracle, the whole world. Nothing is an accident to her, nothing a coincidence. She accepts the world as it is, fights to be a part of it. She doesn't sit around calculating probabilities and possibilities of something happening or not happening."

He finishes his monologue breathing heavily. In a way, he has a point. Cat is sensitive. That much is obvious. However, wooing is out of the question. We brought her those silly flowers because she got hurt, not because we wanted to ask her out on a date.

"It's been years, Stefan," he says defeatedly. "When are you going to let it go?"

I know we're not talking about Cat any longer. He wants me to let go of Xena, to forget that she ever existed. What he doesn't understand is that it's not the love I can't forget. It's the guilt of her death.

"I can't let go of something that is my fault."

"Seriously, again with this," he shakes his head at me. "We've all told you it wasn't your fault. You're not a god!"

"Be that as it may, I could have saved her. I didn't."

"Stefan, don't be – "

"If you disagree on my choice of mate, you are free to express your concern," I reply, my nostrils flaring.

The last thing I wanted to discuss right now was Xena.

"In the meantime, we should speak with Taarus about the raven. Perhaps he knows more."

Vlad doesn't say anything. He doesn't have to. I turn around and leave his room, feeling strangely certain that for the first time in ages, I felt like he didn't understand me.

Chapter 15
Cat

I couldn't find Taarus upon my return with the raven, so I put him in a box in my room and shoved it under the bed. Somehow, the rest of the day passed by without me even remembering it.

That night, I am visited by nightmares worse than any I've ever had before. I see my father burning in a sea of fire, with demons tearing off his flesh with their teeth. He is screaming in pain. I try to run over to him to help, but I realize that I'm also chained to the wall. All I can do is watch in horror the sight before me, as tears stream down my face.

I wake up with a loud gasp, staring at the nothingness around me. I press the tips of my fingers to my eyes. They feel wet. I've been crying. I breathe heavily, in an effort to remind my body as well as my mind that it was just a bad dream. A horribly bad dream, but just a dream, nonetheless. It had no power over me when I was awake.

Only, somehow it had. I can't escape that well known ominous feeling that something horrible is about to happen. I just don't know what. It is then that I remember the box under my bed. I hesitate for a few moments, consciously reminding myself that I am an adult now and there is no such thing as monsters under the bed. I just need to look under it and that's that. Only, that's not how it works.

In the darkness of the night, we all revert back to our childhood selves, especially after a horrible nightmare. Finally, I decide to rip it like a band aid. Quickly. I bend down, grab the box with my eyes closed and then sit back on the bed again.

My eyes are still closed. A part of me has that irrational fear that if I open my eyes, that monster will get me. But, if I keep my eyes closed, I can't see it, and it can't see me either. It's funny how the mind of a child works.

I light the oil lamp next to my bed and welcome the light. I see the faint outlines of the few pieces of furniture in my room and recognize them all. Shapes in the darkness have lost all their power of threat in the light. I open the box and look at the bird. It is starting to smell. My nose frowns, and I know that tomorrow, I'll need to bury it, unless I want my entire room to smell like death. That definitely won't help with my nightmares.

Then, I remember that Taarus sometimes can't sleep either. Perhaps I could find him in the library, like that first night. Closing the lid on the box, I tiptoe out of my room and head straight for the library. When I reach it, I see a light flickering underneath. Slowly, I open the door, my eyes searching for Taarus' face.

I find him in exactly the same spot as the previous time. He lifts his gaze to welcome me, and I notice that he is holding the exact same book. The book of Thoth.

"Good evening," I greet him, although I'm not really sure what to say in the middle of the night.

"Evening is long gone, but morning is nowhere in sight," he smiles. "What is it then?"

"Nighttime?" I wonder, taking a step closer to him. He puts the book in his lap, focusing all of his attention on me.

"A time when anything is possible," he explains. "The time when light and darkness intertwine, this world and the other."

"What does that mean?"

"That means that the dreams you have on a night such as this one might be telling you more than you're ready to hear."

I remember my horrible nightmare. "Oh, God, I hope not."

"I take it you had an unpleasant dream then, which is keeping you up once again?" he smiles kindly.

"Sort of," I nod. "But, that's not the only reason why I'm here."

"Oh?" he asks, and only then notices the box in my hands.

"I found this when I returned from my walk today."

I approach him and place the box in his lap. He doesn't take it, nor does he try to open it. His eyes are firmly focused on mine, as if waiting for me to tell him everything before the mystery of the box is revealed.

"It's a dead bird," I blurt out.

"A dead bird?" he repeats.

"A raven, actually," I nod. "And... someone tore off his beak."

If he knows what that is supposed to mean, he doesn't show it. Instead, he proceeds to pick up the lid and opens the box. His head bends down. He inhales deeply. I frown, knowing that it smells pretty nasty, but he doesn't seem to mind. He remains like that for a few seconds, then closes the box again.

"Sit down, Ecaterina," he tells me gravely, and it reminds me of my father's voice when he had something crucial to tell me, something that might save my life one day.

I do as he bids.

"Where did you go today?"

"I... went for a walk," I say, my cheeks revealing me for the liar that I am. "Just for some fresh air."

He gives me a look which assures me that he knows exactly where I went. I feel that old, familiar embarrassment back when I was a child, and I knew I'd done something wrong. My cheeks flare up, but I try to remain calm, biting the inside of my cheek.

"We all choose our paths here," he tells me calmly. "There is no punishment. We all understand the rules and we abide by them. But, most of those rules apply to some of us, and not to others."

He speaks cryptically, but I think I know what he's referring to. He doesn't want to point the finger of blame and call me a liar. He wants me to admit that on my own. Why is everything in this place hard to do?

"I've broken a rule that was mine to obey," I look down as I speak. He is silent, waiting for me continue, to tell him everything, and I feel the strangest urge to do so, as if that will somehow make everything just a tad little bit better. "I went to the outskirts of the Wailing Woods to pick flowers for Willow."

"I have seen that bouquet," he nods. "It is lovely. But, was it worth the risk?"

"I guess not," I admit. "Also, I put others at risk here. I am more sorry for that."

"Spoken like a true member of the pack," he smiles, and I see no judgment in his gaze, for which I'm grateful. Then, he tells me the words that all of us want to hear at some point in our lives, even if that isn't true. "It's all right."

He takes my hand into his. The touch feels warm, reassuring. This truly is a place of forgiveness, understanding and sympathy. Little by little, I see why someone would want to stay here indefinitely and not go back to the outside world where insecurity and fear rule. Here, life makes sense because it is all about forgiveness. But, I guess for some forgiveness comes easier than for others.

"As for the bird you found... it is a warning," he tells me something I've already sensed, only on a subconscious level. Why would I have taken it with me otherwise?

"A warning?" My throat dries up, as the cold claw of fear taps me on the back. "About what?"

"Birds are considered messengers," he explains, letting go of my hand. "Some birds, like the dove or the eagle, represent symbols and messages of peace. Others, like the vulture or the raven are called the Angels of Death. The fact that someone left a dead raven by our doorstep, meant for you to find, means that death is near."

"But, why would that someone tear off the poor bird's beak?"

"Because the bird mustn't speak. And, neither must you."

"Speak?" I frown. "About what?"

He shrugs. "A secret of some sorts. Isn't that the only thing one cannot speak of?"

"But, I don't know any secrets."

"So, you think, but someone is certain that you know something."

"And, they'll kill me for it?"

"Not as long as you are here," he assures me gently. "There is magical protection on this place, which is keeping us safe. As you can see, the bird was left on the outer side of the door. Whoever left it there knew that was as far as he could go. I would advise you not to leave the Hermitage in the next several days, just until we see what is happening and if there really is any threat behind this."

"That means I can't go mushroom picking with Stefan and Vlad?" I ask.

"That would be the best for now, yes," he nods.

I don't like it, but the only thing I can do is agree. Also, I've heard of this magical protection, but I thought that it belonged to the olden times. Taarus must be special to still have permission to use the light magic to keep this place safe.

But, before I can ask him anything else, he is already up and headed for the door. He turns to me, then hesitates. I sense there is more to this conversation than he wants to tell me right now.

"Good night, Ecaterina," he finally whispers, then disappears.

I inhale deeply, wondering what my next step could be. I have no idea, because honestly, I have no idea what is going on. I just received a warning to keep quiet about something. But, what?

I tiptoe back to my room, but all I manage to do is stare at the ceiling, until the first morning light illuminates the darkness around me.

Chapter 16
Cat

I only manage to fall asleep in the early hours of the morning, so I skip breakfast. At around noon, I am woken up by a knock on the door. I roll my eyes at whoever it is on the other side. I was told that I wouldn't need to go mushroom picking, so I figured I'd go help out Willow in the kitchen when I get up. However, now it's seems there's a rush of some sort.

"Yes?" I call out, my voice still raspy.

"Can I come in?"

I recognize Stefan's voice immediately. I quickly get up and sit on the bed, leaning onto the pillow. I don't know what he wants, but somehow, I want to find out.

"Uhm, yeah, come in," I reply, and instantly the door opens.

The first thing I sense is his scent. Musky. Muscular. Manly. It's filling my chest, my nostrils, my insides like cologne. I meet his steel blue eyes, and it seems to me that he senses my scent, too. It is just the nature of the wolf. That is how wolves recognize each other. The eyes can always lie, but the nose never.

My eyelids flutter open at him, as he tries a slightly awkward smile. Still, it looks amazing. He flashes a row of those pearly whites and all I can do is just smile in return. It's incredible how weak-kneed someone's smile can make you, someone you've been trying hard not to think about, and yet, this makes you think about them even more. I've been all about contradictions these days.

"Are you alright?" he asks softly instead of a greeting. "Your leg?"

"It's fine," I glance down at my feet, still hiding under the covers.

I can't take my eyes off of him, while all my instincts tell me to look away. His raven black hair is parted to the side, but those eyes... I can't seem to get enough of them. They appear as if they can see right through me, through any wall I've tried to build around myself, refusing to let anyone in.

I've lost all those I loved. I've lost a home. I'm too vulnerable to even consider getting close or attaching myself to someone. My mind knows this very well, but my heart is pretending like it doesn't.

"I just couldn't sleep last night," I shrug, trying to sound casual. "I spent the whole night at the library."

"With Taarus?" he suddenly asks.

"Uhm, yes," I nod, blinking up at him. "How did you know?"

"Taarus spends most of his nights at the library, reading the book of Thoth."

"When does he sleep then?" I wonder.

"There was a point in the past when I doubted he even slept at all," he confided. "But, of course, he sleeps. We all do. He just needs less than the rest of us. Much less. Did you want to talk to him about something?"

My instinct urges me to dig more deeply into this. I feel like he knows more than he's saying but doesn't want to ask questions directly. The book of Thoth is something all shifters are familiar with, but mainly the basics. We know what it is and what it can do. We also know that it needs to be kept safe from evil hands, because all hell could break loose if the book is lost or used for evil purposes.

"No," I shake my head. "I told you, I couldn't sleep, so I figured I'd just go to the library and read something until sleep comes."

"I see," he replies, but I still see that hesitation and confusion crackling away in the air between us. "I... I have to tell you something."

"Tell me what?" I watch his jaw tighten, as curiosity rises inside of me.

I can hear my own heartbeat, my inhales and exhales, as I wait. His eyes are on me, drinking me in. What is this effect he has on me?

I tried my best to keep him at a distance. I tried not thinking about him. I even tried being quiet around him, just so we wouldn't get closer, but it seems that fate had different plans. It keeps bringing us together no matter how hard we try to stay apart.

"I followed you yesterday," he says it while clearing his throat, so I almost didn't hear him properly. But, I know what that means. He's seen everything.

"You... but, why?" I wonder.

"I saw you sneak out the main entrance," he explains. "And, I knew from the look on your face that you weren't going to do something smart, but exactly the opposite."

I pout. "I don't need to be looked after, you know. I'm a big girl who can take pretty good care of herself."

"While you are here, consider yourself protected by all of us," he corrects me. "It's not just you I would have protected. I would have gone after anyone with the same look on their face."

A part of me doesn't like that he's comparing me to everyone else. That means that he doesn't consider me special in any way. I'm just like the rest of them. I feel even a little insulted, although I'm not supposed to be. I keep reminding myself that this man doesn't owe me anything, neither do I owe him. So, why does it feel that there is some inexplicable connection between us every time he sends that steel blue gaze my way?

"I also saw the bird," he adds silently.

"You did?" I'm taken a little aback, but it does make sense. If he followed me to the outer edge of the Wailing Woods and back, then of course he saw me pick up the dead raven.

"Was that what you went to talk to Taarus about?"

"Yes," I admit. "But, I wasn't lying about the sleeping part. I really wasn't able to sleep."

"I believe you," he nods, and for some reason, I appreciate knowing that he's on my side, and not here to tell me what a stupid thing I've done. I know that myself. I don't need to be reminded of it. "I suppose he explained what the meaning of the bird is."

"He did," I confirm, shifting a little in the bed, and considering even getting out, but instead I stay where I am. The covers are providing some kind of a physical barrier, as if such a thing is necessary.

His presence, and more so his closeness is waking up all sorts of confusing emotions inside of me. I want to run to the window and open it, to allow in the smells from the outside, just so I won't have to smell his fragrance any longer. It confuses me. It makes me want to get closer to him and pull away at the same time.

"And, I'm going to tell you exactly what I told him," I continue, in hopes of keeping distance from him, although it's becoming increasingly difficult, "I don't have any secrets that I'm keeping. Maybe it was meant for someone else."

"Such things are never mistaken," he shakes his head at me. "They reach those they are supposed to reach."

The way he looks at me both exhilarates and frightens me at the same time. I see a magic in those eyes the likes of which I've never seen before. The wolf inside of me reacts instantly. I feel a surge of need, of want and my energy is overflowing. I try to calm it down, but it's almost impossible.

"Then, I must be stupid or something because I must know something I don't even know, I know," I say feeling ridiculous, but it's worth it, because he smiles, and the tension is slightly less tangible.

Before, I doubted Stefan even knew how to smile, but making a fool of yourself is bound to make anyone smile. In the end, it's worth it, because his smile is like the sun, warm and overpowering.

"That can mean only one thing," he says mysteriously, his eyes burning with a strange fire.

"What is that?" I wonder, curiously.

"It means that you don't know yourself as well as you think you do."

I nod. I mean, I don't want to insult him or make him angry, but he didn't tell me anything new.

"Isn't that the case with everyone?"

"Not everyone was given a dead bird for a warning," he reminds me of something I doubt I'll ever forget.

"Now you sound like Vlad," I frown.

"I can't keep his bad influence at bay all the time, now can I?" he smiles.

I've never seen him like this, casual and even joking. Still, I can tell that beneath all this nonchalance lies something grave, something he's not telling me yet or maybe something I myself am not aware of. It feels like an ominous cloud that has been following me from the place I once considered a home, all the way here. I can see it in the distance, but it is still too far away for it to pose any serious threat. Now that I have received a very tangible threat, perhaps that cloud might be bringing forth a storm sooner than I thought it would.

"You are here, in the best place to get to know yourself, Cat," he continues. "You need to understand the inner workings of your mind and heart, how you love, how you hate, how you experience happiness and grief, and even the things which might cause you pain to remember them."

A jolt of ache rushes through me and I immediately remember my father. I lower my gaze, because I feel if I look at Stefan, he will be able to see right through me. I still haven't reached that stage when I am comfortable talking about my past. I don't know if I ever will be. I suppose these things come in time. The past hurts less the more time passes. It's a life's truth. Only, it is easier said than done, waiting for the pain to lessen.

"It is no shame to feel pain," he tells me softly. It is then I raise my eyes to his and see for the first time that he is speaking from experience. He knows what it feels like to lose someone dear, someone close. "We've all lost someone we loved."

"Even you?" I ask, although I already know the answer. I am asking merely because I want to continue this conversation, as this is the closest I've felt to him since I've met him.

Strangely, I want to be even closer to him. He frightens me and thrills me at the same time. I want to know what makes him tick.

"All of us have," he nods.

The look on his face tells me that we've crossed over from casual chitchat into very serious territory. A part of me knows it might be an imposition to ask about his loss. Then, I remember that he knows all about mine. So, if it isn't anything to be ashamed of, then he could share it with me.

"What happened?" I ask, before my brain can turn on the smartest of my grey cells.

I wasn't supposed to ask. I feel like a curious little child who has no idea where to draw the line. Sometimes, that is all I am. But, it's children who always ask the most innocent questions, without any pretense. Their minds and hearts are pure. Maybe there is still the remnant of that pure child somewhere inside of me, aching to get out.

He lifts his gaze to mine, and his startlingly blue eyes seem cold. For a moment, I believe that he won't talk to me ever again, that he will just get up and leave, without a single word. But, his lips part and the words start spilling out of him like a waterfall.

"It's a story as old as time," he starts. "A greedy leader who didn't care about his clan and the uprising that followed, which cost us far more than we were expecting. We underestimated his strength. We didn't know that he had access to the dark magic, and that it was the source of his true power. None of our wolves could even touch him. He killed many of us. The rest of us were outcast, because he knew that if we stayed there, we would eventually find a way to kill him."

"Is he still alive?"

"I don't think so," he shakes his head. "I don't think about him at all. He belongs to another life I used to live, one I don't want to go back to."

"At least you managed to escape with your brother," I remind him of the silver lining.

"He found his way out himself," he explains. "We separated on the very night of the escape, and I honestly believed I would never see him again. Fortunately, I was wrong. But, that is not the reason I can't sleep at night."

"What is the reason then?" I sense a menacing truth rising to the surface.

"Xena."

The sound of a woman's name immediately makes my heart react in a way I don't like, in a way I think is inappropriate for the situation. I shouldn't be jealous. I shouldn't. And, yet I am and there is not a damn thing I can do about it.

I want to ask who she is. I want to know all about this mystery woman who still keeps Stefan awake, but I don't. My green-eyed monster chooses to be patient and to allow him to tell the story on his own terms.

"She was my mate," he says, and the green-eyed monster roars inside of me. Has he bonded with her? If he has, then he is off limits. "We didn't bond yet, but we were planning to during her first shift."

I always considered that pretty unfair. Men get to shift as many times as they'd like, choosing their mate only when they are ready. Women on the other hand need to make that choice the first time they shift. It's an old tradition, and an overly patriarchal one, but no one seems to challenge it and it just keeps on going.

Once again I remember the man I almost bonded myself to. Tidus. That piece of shit who was too busy saving his own ass, even if that meant throwing me to the wolves. Literally. I can't imagine I ever wanted such a coward for a mate. I make a conscious effort to come back to the present moment and the man before me. How different he is than Tidus, how much braver. The two men couldn't be compared for the simple fact that Tidus wasn't a man at all. He was a mere boy disguised in the body of a young man.

"She was by my side when we decided to leave," he continues. "We only had the light of the moon to go by. We waded through the river, all the time I held her by the hand, I wouldn't let go, although it was difficult for her to keep up. But, we had to keep going, because if we got caught, we would both die. We went through the Wailing

Woods, and finally reached the Malefic Mountains. She was exhausted. We couldn't stop to rest, not until we were here safely. So, I pushed her to keep on going."

He pauses, and I sense that this is where the story becomes difficult to tell. My heart feels his burden, because it is the same. It feels like someone ripped out a part of our insides and threw it out on the dirt, with you knowing that you will never be able to take it back. So, I allow him to take his time.

"We started climbing the mountain, up the path. You remember it?"

"Yes," I nod.

I almost slipped and fell into the gorge. That was the second time I felt like I'd cheated death. But, I keep this to myself.

"I was behind her, helping her up. I could tell she was breathing with difficulty. She needed to rest, but I urged her to keep on going. Then, her leg slipped, but her hand grabbed on to a rocky edge, holding on tightly. I climbed up over her, reaching out, wanting to grab her by the hand and help her, but she couldn't hold on. Her own body was too heavy, and she was exhausted. She fell." He looks down at his feet, then back up at me with a blank stare. "I wake up at night hearing her scream my name as she keeps falling. The sound of her body hitting rock bottom. Then, silence."

"Stefan, I..." I don't even know what to say. I press my hand to my lips in shock and disbelief.

"I keep thinking that if only we stopped to rest, she wouldn't have been so exhausted, she would've been able to hold on and she wouldn't have fallen. So, you see this is all my fault. I deserve to have sleepless nights and to be plagued by nightmares, because I failed the only person I was supposed to keep safe."

"No, you mustn't think that," I shake my head at him, but I'm still in shock and it's hard to get my message across. "This wasn't your fault."

He inhales deeply. "I didn't share this story so you would make me feel better about myself. I was actually planning on doing the exact opposite."

"Make me feel better?" I frown.

"Vlad is better at these things," he says, raking his fingers through his hair, then turning away from me and walking over to the window.

I finally get up from the bed and walk over to him. My hand trembles as I reach to touch his shoulder. As soon as he feels my touch, he turns around.

"I know what it feels when you think that you are responsible for the death of a loved one," I assure him. "My father challenged Kaige because he wanted a better future for me and the rest of my clan. He did it for selfless reasons. Just like you wanted a better future for Xena, even if that was away from your home. She followed you because for her, there was no other way. She trusted you. If you planned on making her your mate, then she must have loved you. And, what happened was a tragedy, a horrible, horrible tragedy, but it was no one's fault. Sometimes, life is just a shitstorm."

He presses his lips together but remains silent. He nods, then walks around me, and heads for the door. I keep hoping that he will stop, but he proceeds to open the door, and a few moments later, I am left alone, in shock and disbelief.

He said I need to get to know myself. At this point, I'm not sure what's more difficult: getting to know myself or Stefan?

Chapter 17
Cat

Just a few minutes after Stefan leaves my room, Willow barges in looking a little breathless. She presses her hand to her bustling chest and stops to take a breath before she tells me what she came for. I watch as her red cheeks revert to their usual, sun-kissed hue and her green eyes assure me that she didn't come to just wish me a good morning, or good day at this point.

"Taarus needs to speak to you," she says in one breathless go.

"OK," I lift my eyebrow at her in wonder. "But, I don't see the urgency."

"You have fifteen minutes to get there, that's all I can say," she shrugs her shoulders.

I see she's not wearing her usual white robes with an apron. Today, she's in a lovely lavender colored dress, and her grey hair is braided in the back.

"OK, I'll go immediately," I nod, rubbing my eyes with the tips of my fingers, incredulous at the way this day has started, and it's just noon.

I'm just wondering what else is awaiting me.

"When I'm done there, I'd like to come and help you in the kitchen," I smile. "Taarus said I can't go mushroom picking anyway, so I might as well make myself useful to you."

"I do appreciate the offer, kid," her eyes light up at me in such a way that I want to wrap my arms around her, "but, I doubt you'll be done with Taarus so quickly."

"Done?" I frown. "What do you mean? What does he want with me?"

"I honestly can't tell you," she says, closing up a pretend zipper across her full lips. "But, in all seriousness, you need to get there right now."

"Alright, alright," I lift my hands in mock surrender, then quickly change, and I'm already being pushed out of my room and down the corridor towards Taarus' study.

"There," she finally says, still by my side. "Just remember to relax, OK? We've all done it."

"Done what?" I'm feeling increasingly suspicious by now, even more so because she obviously won't tell me a thing. "What the heck is going on here, Willow?"

"Gotta go, kid," she leans over and presses her lips to my cheek, then disappears down the hallway.

I sigh before lifting my hand to knock on Taarus' door, and the moment I do so, I hear his voice from inside inviting me in. I do as I am instructed and the moment I push the door open, I see he's also not wearing his usual robe. This one is more complex, with a silver belt that hangs to the side and a cape which is embroidered with golden threads. He looks like a wizard from the olden days, the likes of which don't even exist anymore... or so I thought.

"Ah, Ecaterina," he smiles upon seeing me, and his beard reveals the thinness of his lips as well as the perfect alignment of his teeth. "Thank you for coming."

"Well, I wasn't left with much choice," I smile back.

"Indeed," he seems amused by the whole thing, whatever it is. "That is because the potion needs to be taken immediately."

"Potion?" My brows furrow. "What potion?"

"The potion that is to reveal your wolf, of course."

"Wait, wait," I wave my arms apprehensively in the level of my chest. "You want me to shift here, for the first time?"

"No, no, goodness no," he chuckles, walking over to a wooden table by his bookshelf, and taking a small jar that rests on it. There is a strangely blue liquid inside. He walks back to me and offers me the jar. "You will have a vision, and this vision will reveal your inner wolf to you."

This was all making no sense. Why do I need to drink God knows what, when I can just shift? Unless he was giving me something else entirely. But, why? Would he lie? Would Willow lie? I didn't think so, but this whole thing still smelled fishy.

The jar still hovered in the air between us.

"The potion is good for only a few minutes longer," he explains. "That is why Willow rushed you over. The ingredients of this potion are very special and very strong. For the best effects, you need to take it within 15 minutes of it being made."

"What will it do to me?"

I'm still suspicious. No one here mentioned any drinking of weird potions.

"I told you, nothing," he repeats. "You'll just have a vision. Think of it as a dream. Your body will be suspended here. Do not worry, I shall remain here to oversee the process. It is your mind that will undergo this journey, not your body."

I glance at the same table from which he took the jar. There is also an hourglass, counting the fifteen minutes, I suppose. More than half of the sand has already seeped down.

"You may refuse, of course," Taarus suddenly says, as if he just remembered that option.

I can sense the fight inside of me. I know they've taken me in and provided shelter, but what if that potion is something else entirely, something that might harm me? What about the dead bird? What about the threat? Who sent it and why?

A million questions swarm inside my mind. A million questions and not a single answer.

Angrily, I grab the jar from him and pour it all down my throat, swallowing with a loud, mockingly satisfied clacking of the tongue.

"There," I say, giving him back the empty jar. "Now what?"

"Now, we wait," he smiles. "It shouldn't take long for the process to start."

I look around the room. It is Taarus' private room, which I've never been in. We usually have our unplanned talks during the night in the library. This place is more or less the same. Lots of books. Only one window which doesn't let in nearly enough light. That's what you get for making a home inside an actual mountain.

I look down at my feet and realize that the ground is grassy.

"How do you make grass grow in here?" I wonder, lifting my gaze, but I realize that I'm alone. Taarus is gone. "So much for your promise," I say it out loud, not caring whether he'll take offense or not.

I look down again, and a few silvery flowers pop out of the dark greenery. I go down to my knees, pressing my open palms to the grass. It even smells like grass. Was it here when I came, before I took the potion? Is this the process Taarus spoke about, seeing things that aren't here?

I feel something inside of me stir. It's not completely unpleasant, but it does feel like there is a cage inside of me and something is itching to come out after a long, long time of being held under a lock and key.

I turn my gaze to the corner of the room, when I catch a shadow of something crawling along the walls. But, the moment I look in that direction, the shadow moves, and it keeps moving, always away from my direct gaze, but always visible in the corner of my eye.

A strange energy fills me to the brim, as the shadow flickers all around me now. It's gotten closer. I quickly look at it, and this time, it doesn't move. It is a shapeless effervescent cloud, hovering. Then, slowly, it starts to form a shape. I see a wolf's head, a muzzle, a pair of eyes, a body. But, it keeps shifting, so it's never the same wolf. One moment it's growling. The other it's grinning.

She disappears from sight, only to nudge her head against my back so forcefully I jump forward in fright.

"Argh!" I shout.

I hear a soft growl, and I can't tell if she's angry or amused. She. It's a wolf. My wolf. Is it me? Is she a part of me or am I a part of her?

She moves around me, brushing the bottom of my legs. I can feel her energy intertwined with mine. I want to touch her, but I dare not extend my hand yet. She's still a cloud, silvery and white. Maybe my mind is still too weak to fully flesh her out. I wonder if I will be able to by the end of the vision.

I stand frozen in one place, watching the wolf cloud. She floats in the air, lowering her head to the flowers. I think she likes them as much as I do. I see one of her paws forming. She presses it onto the flower, which doesn't bend under the weight.

Suddenly, I see my father's image at the window.

"Father!" I shout, running over there.

By the time I press my hand to the window, he's gone. But, she is here. My wolf. Her muzzle is on my shoulder. I can feel the warmth of her breath. I turn slowly to look at her. She has fleshed out slightly more. I see the bristles of her hair. The silvery fur.

However, her eyes are still formless as is most of her body. Her hackles rise, as if she's seen him, too. She knows who it was. How could she not?

"Was that really father?" I ask both myself and her.

She pulls away. She is no longer on my shoulder, and I already miss her. I turn around, and I'm no longer in Taarus' room. It is the bonfire of my father's death, burning bright. I smell the blood. The dirt. I feel the hands holding onto me, not letting me go. But, I look to my sides, I'm still alone. She isn't here.

"Stop constraining her," I suddenly hear Taarus' voice.

So, he is here. The thought soothes me. He hasn't left me to my own devices. I won't die in this vision, which is strangely, my biggest fear.

He's telling me to stop constraining her. She is the one rattling the cage, eager to come out, and I am the one stopping her. Only, I'm not doing anything. Then, it hits me. Is she the secret I am not supposed to let out?

I hear a soft snarl in my right ear. That same warm breath. The smell of death on her teeth. Is that really me?

The fire crackles loudly and I see Kaige's face in the flames, forming the rest of his body. He's standing right before me, staring me down.

"You are weak, just like your father," he laughs.

The wolf growls more softly, but much more resiliently. I look down. I see all her paws, which she is using to step on the newly blossomed silver flowers in the grass. My hand feels the softness of the petals she has just crumpled. Is her touch mine, too? Can she feel what I feel?

Raw energy crackles through my body, like electricity. The fire before me explodes. I almost shriek at the sight, fearing that it might burn me up alive, but she is here, fully fleshed out. She is no longer a smoky vision, but a majestic animal with white silvery fur and fangs which she bares to protect me from Kaige.

I recognize her need, because it is my own. Her energy bursts out of me, our souls becoming one. The fire takes on a cobalt hue, as the flames flicker around like dancing tongues, but I'm not afraid any longer. Not when she is by my side.

Her paws are my own. Her claws are my own. I growl with her voice. Her own vocal cords tremble inside my throat. The beautiful silvery paleness of her fur is so intense it burns my eyes.

I feel ready to attack anyone who wishes to do me any harm, but before I do that, a bright explosion blossoms all around me, so brilliant I have to close my eyes, allowing darkness to engulf me whole.

Chapter 18
Cat

When I open my eyes, I realize it's the middle of the night and I'm in my bed. When did I get back here? Did I walk or was I brought here? I have no memory of the previous several hours, actually of the whole day. I remember going to see Taarus, drinking that potion and then having such a trip that I think everyone in Woodstock would envy me.

My head roars loudly, objecting to me being awake. I feel like I'm in a weird daze, and even though I'm tired, I probably won't be going to sleep again. Not that I want to. What I do want to do is make some sense of what I've just experienced.

I try to get up, and once more, my entire body opposes this action. Three oil lamps around me shed more than enough light for me to see that I am alone in my room, and at the same time, I feel like I'm not. I feel that same hazy, dreamlike, cloudy presence. Maybe it's been here all along, only I wasn't able to feel it. Now I can.

I see her in the dancing of the shadows around me. I want to call out to her, get acquainted properly, but for now, maybe it's best to just admire her from afar, until I figure out what we are to each other.

I plant my feet firmly onto the cold floor, and it tenses me a little, enough to sharpen my mind and focus it. I know what I want to do now. I need to speak to Taarus and ask him about this whole vision. What did he know about it, about me? And, why is my wolf white and silvery grey, and not like all the other ones I've seen shift?

I listen to the sound of silence around me. Every once in a while, there is a barely audible snarl meant for my ears alone. But, no matter how quickly I turn to that side, there's still no one there. She's gone, or perhaps she has moved so quickly that I couldn't see her. I have to know more. I just have to.

I walk down the dark hallway like an apparition. That's what I would probably look like to anyone unlucky to open the door at that point in the night. But, I don't care. I'm rushing to the library, because that is the only place where I can have my questions answered and make some sense of all this.

The entire time, I can't get the image of my wolf out of my head. She is absolutely stunning. I never imagined that a shifter wolf could look that breathtaking. She oozes dominance and confidence, and only appears when she wants to. Is it possible that this is me? That I could ever be like her? The possibility of that makes my heart skip a beat.

I finally reach the door to the library, and for a moment, I think I hear voices coming from inside. Is Taarus in there with Willow? That is my first thought, because I've come to know that she is not only his friend, but his partner as well as confidant. It wouldn't be such a strange notion for them to meet up in the middle of the night to talk about things which they can't talk about during the daytime.

I knock on the door gently, and the conversation inside dies out. I wait to be called in, but I hear nothing. So, I knock again. Instead of Taarus' voice welcoming me inside, the door suddenly swings open, and I see Vlad standing there.

"Oh, hey," he grins. "I thought you'd be sleeping like a log after the vision."

I frown. "Does everyone know everything around here?"

He moves to the side to let me in, and I walk past him. He closes the door behind me. There is a small fireplace in the corner, and the fire is gently flickering. Although it's not cold outside, when you're deep inside a mountain, it doesn't matter which month of the year it is. You feel cold all the time.

I walk over to the fire and stretch my arms closer, enjoying the soft flickering sounds. Only then do I notice that Stefan is seated on the chair where Taarus usually sits. His right foot is resting on his left knee. his night black hair is pulled sleek, while his head is tilted, resting on the back of the armchair.

"What are you guys doing here?" I ask.

"We could be asking you the same thing," Vlad snickers.

"I still asked first," I reply, glancing at the bottle and two glasses on the small table. "Celebrating something?"

"We're alive," Vlad shrugs. "When you're alive and well, there's so much to celebrate."

I frown not because I'm annoyed at Vlad, but because I'm both annoyed and amused. I just wish this goddamn headache would ease up on me.

"Are you going to answer my question seriously?" I turn to Stefan, who looks even more mysterious in the darkness as the firelight flickers on his face.

"It seems like the library is where insomniacs meet," he tells me.

"What? I'm no insomniac," Vlad gives us a mock evil eye. "I just like drinking at night, so no one sees me." He proceeds to take one of the glasses, which is filled with ruby red liquid and takes a sip. "To your health, my dear."

"Instead of drinking to her health, you should be offering her a drink," Stefan comments, with his glass still politely in place.

"After that potion Willow concocted? No way in Hell," I shake my head at the bottle which looks like it contains blood. That is probably the last thing I want to be drinking right now.

"This is actually the antidote to that," Vlad grins.

"The antidote?" I grimace. "You mean to tell me what I drank initially was poison?"

I swear most of the time I have no idea if he's joking or not. Still, it makes up for great fun. As long as you've got Vlad here, you won't be bored.

Vlad chuckles. "Gosh, you're so easy."

I'm annoyed, but still equally amused. And, why does Vlad look the cutest when he's chuckling like that, so mischievously?

"Of course not," Stefan quickly adds. "Vlad is just trying to tell you, in his own very special way, that we've all drunk it upon our arrival here. It helps the mind process the trauma that we've all been through, and also, in cases such as yours, when the first shift is yet to happen, it helps you get to know your wolf before the moment comes."

That actually makes a lot of sense. I've heard that the first shift is the hardest. In rare cases, shifters died before even finishing the process. My father told me about that. They were torn limb to limb, inside to outside, because there was some discrepancy between them and their wolf, and the shift proved to be destructive for the host. I always thought that was just scary stuff to keep me in line, but the more time passes by, I realize that my father was only telling me the truth. It's my own fault for not taking it seriously enough.

"You know what?" I lift my chin at the bottle. "I think I'll try that bloody drink you got there."

"Here," Vlad immediately offers me his glass, which is half full. "You can take mine."

Is he testing me?

I smirk, taking the glass from his hand and downing the drink in one go. I give him back the empty glass. The grin on his face is priceless.

"Seems I have misjudged you," he says, with a mischievously raised eyebrow. "More?"

But, before I can answer, I feel a tidal wave of warmth overpower me. It feels like a warm breeze and a cold waterfall at the same time, and the sensations keep alternating.

Hot. Cold. Hot. Cold.

My mind opens up like a double window to welcome the nonexistent sun in this room. Somewhere, deep inside my mind, I hear the snarl of my wolf. She's awake. She hasn't left me.

My vision sharpens, and I can suddenly read more than half of the book titles, which rest on the opposite side of the library. I lift my hand to my eyes, as if I'm seeing it for the first time. I feel like I'm moving too slow, then too fast.

"I see it kicked in already," Vlad chuckles. "No wonder. You drank it in one go. You were supposed to sip it."

"I don't sip stuff," I reply not taking my eyes off of my hands and fingers, which are now floating through the air.

I turn to Stefan. He is still sitting in the armchair, he has just slightly shifted, but I know he hasn't taken his eyes off of me. It burns and cools me down at the same time. I feel like my body is itching, and I want to take off not only my clothes, but my skin as well.

"I... I think I need to sit down for a bit," I say forcing my eyelids to open and stay that way.

But, I'm not sleepy. Just incredibly aroused for some reason. Awakened. Bold. The tips of my fingers are tingling, itching to feel something underneath them.

I sit on the sofa opposite Stefan.

"Get her some water," he tells Vlad.

"I'm fine," I quickly add, with a quick shake of my head. "The drink is just a little rough."

"Just breathe slowly and the effects will disappear," Stefan advises.

"I... I don't think I want them to," I say, seeing her in the corner.

My wolf. Myself. Again, I'm not sure if I'm there in the corner, lurking in the darkness, or is it her? She walks behind Vlad, just a cloud of invisible smoke. I'm not even sure he sees her. He doesn't seem to. She sniffs his hand which is just hanging in the air. He doesn't pull back. She glances over at me, then flutters over to Stefan.

He must sense her... right? How can she be there, without them knowing?

She walks around him, sniffing him as well. She becomes more fleshed out with each passing moment. Then she –

"What are you looking at?" Stefan suddenly asks me, and I realize I'm staring at his crotch, because that is where the she wolf has placed her paw.

"I..." I start, but she's there, pressing on his groin and he's not saying anything.

If he can't see her, then what's the point of me admitting that my wolf is there, groping him?

"Sorry, I'm not looking at you, I'm looking through you," I try the oldest explanation in the book. "I'm just too sleepy, I guess."

That's a lie. I'm not sleepy at all. I'm randy and excited, and for some reason I want my hand to be there, where she has pressed her paw. I swallow heavily as Stefan smiles.

"Maybe we shouldn't have let you drink," he tilts his head a little as he's speaking. The she wolf growls softly. But, it's not even a growl, it's something more primal, more needy.

Then, it happens. It starts off as slight tingling right in the middle of my palm. I scratch it, thinking it's just an itch. Only the sensation intensifies, and I finally realize that she's making me feel what she is feeling – her paw on his cock. And, it's... he's hard. He's aroused.

I can't see it in the dark. Also, he's wearing pants with a wider fit, so even if he does have an erection, I can't tell. I can only feel it because she wants me to feel it.

I pull my hand away, as if I just got burned, but that does nothing. The sensation is still there.

"Are you OK?" Vlad wonders, walking over to me and standing by my side.

"Yes, I'm fine," I manage to muster, feeling a strange heat take over me, starting from my chest, traveling down my belly and finally, pooling right between my thighs.

What the hell is happening? I have no idea. All I know is that I want to stay here, and I want so many things, crazy things, but I know all that is impossible. Why is she even here? Why is she touching him like that?

Vlad leans over, his nose right underneath my right ear, and inhales deeply. I know he can sense my arousal.

I know... because I can sense his as well.

Chapter 19
Cat

When I glance at the she wolf again, she is gone. But, the sensation of Stefan's manhood in my hand is still there. I can't seem to shake it off, to wipe it off... honestly, I'm not even sure I want to.

Maybe I needed her to come out, so she would show me what it is I truly desire, what I couldn't admit even to myself. Stefan still has his gaze on me, and I feel like he is undressing me with it. It's strange, because he's always so calm, so held back. You never know what he's thinking. Only now, I know what we're all thinking. I know what we all want. But, how do you even start something so crazy, so completely unbelievable?

Vlad slowly walks behind me, and gently places his hands on my hips. His touch is warm. There is no more shifting of hot and cold. There is only heat, which is threatening to consume me alive, unless I find a way to release it.

"If I do anything you don't like, tell me to stop, OK?" I hear him whisper, and all I can do is nod.

I can't believe I'm doing this. I feel Vlad's lips on my earlobes, nibling on them, and it feels so good. Stefan is still seated on the armchair, and he is watching us. Honestly, I don't know what is turning me on more: Vlad's touches or Stefan's gaze.

I hear him exhale, and I become even more aware of him, although he is the one not even touching me. Then, suddenly, I remember something.

"What if someone walks in on us?"

I can't believe that this is what I'm worried about, while every one of my senses is heightened to the brim.

"No one will walk in on us," Vlad whispers, and the heat of his breath makes me shiver wildly. "Taarus was here and left a little before you arrived. No one else comes here at night, but us."

"But, what if – "

That is about as much as I get to say, as his voice turns to a decadent rasp in my ear, and it silently promises to make me see heaven tonight. Vlad's hand slips from my waist to my breast, cupping it ever so gently. I'm only wearing a thin t-shirt, which falls all the way to my knees, and just a pair of underwear underneath. Nothing else. My nipples respond to his touch immediately, perking up. He tugs at one, teasing it, and it's an exquisitely sweet painful sensation.

"You're not wearing a bra, are you?" Vlad whispers.

"No," I manage to muster.

He pauses before he continues. "Show us."

I shudder at his order. I swallow heavily, already knowing that I will do it. I will do anything they want me to.

"What should I do?" I ask.

"Take it off," he instructs softly.

I'm not sure if I should be insulted by this or aroused. My mind has already made up its mind which one it prefers. All I can feel is an enormously overpowering rush of desire which is strong enough to bring me to my knees.

Vlad lets go of me, and I'm surrounded by their gaze. Stefan's countenance is grave, as usual. I almost can't tell if he wants to pleasure me or punish me. Maybe in this case, both are acceptable. I know I would accept either from him, just to have him touch me.

Strangely, I trust them both. My she wolf trusts them both. Why else would she nuzzle them and even place her paw on Stefan's crotch? They would never hurt me. All they have done so far was show their care. They saved me. They protect me. I sense there is more than that, but none of us is willing to go there. Maybe it's too soon.

I lower my hands to the hem of my t-shirt, crumpling it up in my hands. I hesitate only for a moment, that familiar heat pooling between my thighs again, and I know what that is. I'm wet. I'm ridiculously horny. I've never felt this way before.

I swing my arms upward in one smooth motion, and my t-shirt flies off of me. Instinctively, I raise my hands to my breasts, hiding them. Stefan smiles with just the corners of his lips, and if he wanted me to drop to my knees right then and there, I would have gladly done it.

"Let us see you," Vlad speaks from behind me, in that baritone which is making me hotter by the second. "Everything."

Not for a single moment does it cross my mind to put the t-shirt back on and to leave the library. Every fiber in my being wants to stay here, and I can't fight the feeling. I grab my underwear with the tips of my fingers and let it fall down, pooling around my ankles. Then, I step out of them, completely naked.

For a moment, I feel slightly chilly, but their hot gazes chase away the cold. I am once again consumed by fiery flames and I don't know how long I can hold on, before I'm burned alive.

Vlad walks over to me, and touches me softly on the shoulders, trailing an invisible line down my back.

"You are so beautiful," he whispers. "Hot like fire."

Gently, his fingers trail down my back, and the sensuality of the touch sends goosebumps up and down my body. I feel powerful and reckless at the same time, vulnerable and strong, wanted and needed. Desired.

His lips land on my neck. It's a teasing touch, promising more. So much more. I love the way they look at me, as if they want to devour me whole. I want to be devoured. My she wolf wants to be devoured. If she trusts them, I trust them, too. But, it's so much more than mere trust.

Vlad's kisses become deeper, wetter. I feel the slipperiness of his tongue on my naked skin, swirling over my flesh, over my collar bone, making my inner thighs tremble for what's to come.

His fingers glide down my upper arms to my elbow, circling over this most unlikely part of my body, yet I love it. It feels that the entire area of my skin is tingling, and they are to blame for it.

"You taste so delicious," Vlad murmurs. "I want to taste every part of your sweet, delectable body. Then, I want to spread your legs, and feel the heat of your inner fire. I want to get lost in it. I want to bury my cock inside your tight little pussy, and watch you drip wet while I fuck your brains out. Would you like that?"

His words shock me. They thrill me. They awaken all sorts of emotions inside of me, and the strangest part? I want all of it, and more. I've never felt anything so intense, so effortlessly fulfilling.

Without thinking, I drop to the ground. My mind is still hazy, but I know it's not the drink. It's the she wolf guiding my every move, telling me what to do, what I want to do, only I was too much of a coward to admit it to myself.

I'm not taking my eyes off of Stefan, nor is he taking his eyes off of me. Slowly, I crawl over to him, on all fours, feeling exactly like my she wolf. I put one hand on his foot, the other on his knee. He doesn't move. He is looking at me with those hot, burning eyes, waiting for me to do it all. And... I love it.

All of my senses are alive, heightened. I inhale deeply as I raise myself to him, spreading his knees apart. The mound on his pants is huge, bulging. I swallow heavily, biting my lower lip. The corner of his lip dances in a half-smile.

I hear Vlad drop to his knees behind me, and his finger trails underneath me, my belly, circling my navel. He brushes his arm against my pussy, and the innocent touch almost makes me explode. He pulls his hand back to himself slowly, his fingers finally resting where I want them to. He is teasing my starving flesh, sliding into me so effortlessly. I moan loudly, trying to keep my knees from buckling.

It's hard to focus on anything else, but I try. Not taking my eyes off of Stefan's, I pull down his pants, not the least bit surprised to see that he's wearing nothing underneath. His cock springs to sight, glorious and thick, ready. My hands are on his inner thighs, caressing him gently, while Vlad's fingers keep sliding in and out of me with increased pressure.

My lips part, and I feel like I'm just a guest in my own body, having no control over what happens, but allowed to feel all the pleasure. I press my lips softly to the tip of Stefan's most intimate, sensitive flesh. I hold his gaze, as my lips curl into an O, and I allow him in deeper.

At that moment, Vlad's hand pulls away and instead, he prods my wet entrance with his thick cock. He teases me at first, just pressing into me, until I can't take it any longer, and I ram into him myself. He slides in all the way, filling me. A breathy moan escapes me, then my mouth falls on Stefan's cock once more, devouring it.

I am mindless as Vlad's thickness makes me quiver. I am in a completely uncontrolled frenzy, all three of us a hot wet mess. Stefan's fingers rake through my hair, grabbing a handful of it, but he doesn't take over. He allows me to pleasure him any way I wish to, and the sensation makes me even wilder.

My tongue is playing with his tip, teasing it, circling around it. I grab his balls into my hand, toying with the sack, feeling his cock twitch and tighten even more inside my mouth, as his tip scrapes against the back of my throat.

"Fuck, you feel so good..." I hear Vlad groan behind me, and that is all it takes for me to come with a strangled cry, my body shivering, trembling with the sheer power of my orgasm. I feel my own juices dripping out of me as Vlad resumes the frenzied tempo. It's like my orgasm only intensified his need. He digs his fingers into my waist and keeps fucking me even harder, while my entire body is still trying to process the remnants of my release.

He suddenly pulls out, and I feel a shower of his cum on my ass cheeks. Stefan's cock still needy pats me on the lips, and I dive once more, sucking him off, delirious with the need to make him cum. After mere seconds, he collapses backward, his head falling and his eyes closing. I feel the thickness of his cum inside my mouth, but I don't stop.

Almost lovingly, I keep kissing the tip of his cock, still dripping beads of cum, lapping them up hungrily. Haziness blurs my eyesight, and I feel once more like at the end of the previous vision.

Did this really happen? Or, was it just the prolonging result of that potion I drank?

Chapter 20
  Cat

I wake up once more in my own bed. The images of the previous day and night come back to me immediately. I gasp silently. Did I really do all that? It feels like a dream, like a part of that vision.

Yes, that must be it. Since the she wolf was there, then it must still have been a part of my vision, right? Right.

I keep reminding myself that I didn't just have sex with two brothers, because that is totally unlike me. I would never do that. No way. Absolutely, positively no way. But, then again, ever since I came here, I feel like I'm someone different, someone new.

In the back of my mind, the wolf snarls softly, as if reminding me of something I've willingly forgotten.

"What is it?" I say out loud, but there is no reply. I am alone in my room, and the rays of the sun enter through my window, telling me it's probably time to get up.

I guess I'm supposed to go to Taarus and talk to him about my vision. Do I even mention that I saw Stefan and Vlad in it? Maybe not. Maybe I just keep that erotic little episode to myself. I'll just tell him about the she wolf and how she revealed herself to me, but I won't tell him that my vision also included a menage.

I inhale deeply, then get out of bed. My stomach is growling. No wonder. I feel like I haven't eaten in days. I quickly get dressed and head over to the kitchen. The dining room is empty, so I'm guessing it's anywhere after breakfast and before lunch time.

I knock on the door to the kitchen. Willow immediately answers from inside, so I open the door.

"Hey, you," she smiles. "How are you feeling?"

"Famished," I answer a little apologetically, to which she chuckles.

"Everyone does," she nods. "Come, I'll whip you up some eggs."

She fetches the eggs from what appears to be a shelf inside the wall. When she opens it, I can feel the onslaught of icy cold air. She grabs the egg carton, then quickly closes the door.

"Colder than a witch's tit in there," she shivers. "Now, lemme see, where is that frying pan?"

She looks around, finally finding what she is looking for. She lights up a small fire and within minutes, we're both seated in the empty dining room, me having a late breakfast and she with a cup of tea in her hands.

She doesn't ask too many questions yet. Instead, she is just waiting for me to finish eating, and I appreciate that. Once my hunger is satiated, I exhale loudly, with a satisfied grin on my face.

"That was awesome," I smile. "Thanks."

"Sure thing. So, have you spoken to Taarus yet?" she wonders, lifting her gaze to me.

It's strange how sometimes, she looks old, almost as old as Taarus, while at other times, like now, she seems just a few years older than me. It's not her face and the fine wrinkles. It's not the loose or tight skin on her body. It's her eyes. It's like she drinks from a fountain of youth every once in a while, and those are the times when she seems unreal, unearthly.

Or, it could also be those concoctions and potions she makes. Maybe she's stumbled onto the recipe for longevity, with the added benefits of looking refreshed and young.

"No," I shake my head. "I went – "

But, then I remember that the events from the library were most certainly parts of the vision as well. I did go in search of him there, but if I mention it, then I'll have to say what happened there. That is, what I imagined happened there.

"Once the vision was over, I woke up in my own bed this morning."

I feel a little bad lying, but it's a white lie. It's meant to keep my emotions secret. Also, I have no idea how the guys would react knowing that I had wet dreams about them.

"So, the vision lasted all day and all night?" she asked, bringing the cup to her lips and taking a sip.

"I guess so," I shrug. "Is that bad?"

"Just unusual," she replies with a smile. "Usually, it's finished by the evening. That's why we start in the morning, so we can supervise what's happening."

"Uhm... supervise?" I swallow heavily.

"Of course," she nods agreeably, and her head bobbles. "Just in case something goes wrong."

"What could go wrong? It's just a vision, no?"

"Well, sometimes, the visions are so strong that they actually make you do what you're seeing inside your mind. You know, like your brain is preventing you from acting out all the stuff you do while dreaming, that is how your body is also being prevented from acting out the stuff you see in your vision. But, like I said, sometimes, your vision is so strong that the brain can't control your body. It gets up, it walks, it... I don't know, if your vision is to jump off a cliff, you might actually do it. So, that's why Taarus and I need to pay close attention to the person undergoing it."

"Has that happened before?" I ask, swallowing heavily.

Did I act out those things? Oh, merciful heavens. I hope not. What will they think of me?

"Maybe once or twice," she admits. "But, we were there to stop her before she went out the door. So, nothing happened."

"You mean, if I headed out the door, you would have prevented me from leaving the room?"

"Absolutely."

I exhale loudly, with relief. At least no one has seen me do it. Now, as for the inner workings of my own mind, they should be ashamed of themselves. Sex with both brothers. Tsk, tsk, tsk.

"Have you seen it?" she asks suddenly.

"My wolf?"

I know what she means, but I'm trying to buy some time. It's difficult to explain in words the vision I had, and it's even more difficult to describe my she wolf.

Breathtaking. Mesmerizing. Fierce. Bold. Unyielding. Demanding.

She is all that and more. But, how do I tell that to someone who hasn't seen her yet? It's impossible, because my she wolf exudes these attributes so effortlessly, as if they were ingrained inside of her.

"Yes," she smiles. "Your wolf. Your spiritual guide. Did she come to you?"

"She did," I beam at her, overcome by the image. "She is... magnificent."

"I didn't doubt that," Willow's face lights up back at me.

Then, I remember how different my wolf is. And, being different isn't always a good thing. It means more trouble, more responsibility, more effort at proving yourself worthy. I wonder if that is what will happen to me.

"But, she is... different," I add, cautiously, waiting for Willow's reaction. She is the one I trust the most here. I feel if I don't tell someone, I might explode.

"What do you mean different?" She inches forward.

I struggle to find the right word. I don't want Willow to think that I deem my wolf unworthy or lacking in any way. That is the last impression I want to make on her. I just wish to find the right words to convey all that my she wolf is, taking into account the fact that she is different.

"She's not a regular wolf, you know, the ones I'm used to seeing. She's grey and silver, white even. But, it's like she's sparkling. I don't know how to explain it."

"A silvery white wolf that sparkles?" she repeats my silly description, but that about covers it. I feel almost as silly as if I've just told her that I've seen a unicorn and now I think they exist.

"Yes," I nod.

I see the deep furrowed line on her forehead, the one that is shown only when she looks her age. Not today. Today, it popped out of nowhere, as if my story somehow aged her with worry, with apprehension, or I don't know what. I just know it doesn't seem good.

She doesn't say anything, so I wave in front of her face.

"Earth to Willow," I try a joke, and she gives me a half-smile. "Are you still here?"

"Yes," she is brought back from her deep thought, but it still seems that she's unwilling to share much about it.

"Any idea why my wolf is silver?"

She sighs. "You know, maybe you'd best take that up with Taarus. He'll explain it far better than I could."

"But, is everything alright? Is there something wrong with me?"

"Wrong?" She leans across the table and takes my hands into hers. "There is absolutely nothing wrong with you, kid. In fact, you are special in more ways than you know."

"Special how?" I wonder.

"I told you, Taarus should be the one to explain it all," she was adamant that she wouldn't reveal more of this.

"Is that why someone is threatening me?" I suddenly remember the bird and how someone is warning me not to reveal a secret.

She opens her lips, but before she can reply, the door suddenly bursts open and Taarus rushes in. He is not wearing his robe, which is highly unlike him. His usually well-combed beard is now knotty and in dire need of some attention. He's wearing a black t-shirt with sleeves up to his elbows, which resemble a pair of bats' wings, as they hang low. I look all the way down and see that his feet are bare, with caked dirt on them.

Both Willow and I look at him in surprise. He would never show himself like this before the rest of us. Even I know that.

"What happened?" Willow is the first one to speak, immediately getting up from her seat.

Taarus glances at her, then looks over at me. His eyes are like blades, cutting into me, and I know that whatever he is going to say next, I won't like it.

"Stefan and Vlad went mushroom picking early this morning," he starts, halting a little as he speaks. Again, that is totally unlike him. Apprehension in me grows as I wait for the punchline. "Only Stefan made it back."

Vlad?

His name echoes inside my mind, as darkness threatens to engulf me. Where is he? What happened?

A cold talon of fear grips my heart. I know the truth.

It's all my fault...

Chapter 21
Stefan

I still don't know how I managed to drag myself back to the Hermitage. My head felt heavier than a boulder. My body was numb. My left eye closed. Bleeding profusely. I left a bloody trail, but I know that I wasn't followed. Even if I was, the light magic guarding this place is still strong enough to keep the evil outside. The only question is how long it will stay up.

Upon arriving back here, I immediately told Taarus what happened. The message was clear. I was left for dead, and Vlad was taken back to the Wailing Woods. Taarus told me to rest for the day, but how can I rest when I don't know what is happening to my brother? Kaige is a beast. He would torture someone just for the fun of it.

I want to get up, but the gaping wound on my head is too fresh. Willow will be coming any moment with her balm. I know it will do its wonders and help me heal faster, but it won't be in time for me to go back and save my brother.

All of a sudden, the door bursts open, and I expect to see Willow. Who I don't expect to see is Cat. She seems frantic, apprehensive. The moment her eyes find mine, she rushes over to me, sitting on the bed. Without any restraint, she takes my hand in hers. I couldn't pull away even if I wanted to. Not after what's happened.

"Are you alright?"

I wish I could answer affirmatively to that question. But, only one glance at me would be enough to know that I'm lying. So, I tell her the truth.

"Honestly, I've been better," I say, trying to focus my gaze, but it's hard.

Taarus has instructed me not to fall asleep. I feel as if that is the single most difficult task I've been given lately: not to fall asleep. I know why. I have a head wound, a pretty serious one. Falling asleep means I might not wake up soon. Or again. So, I focus all of my conscious effort on Cat. Her freckles are even more prominent now. She's not smiling, so I can't see her dimples. But, those eyes are wide and alert. Frightened, too.

"And, Vlad?" she asks almost apologetically, as if it were her who attacked us in the woods, taking Vlad and leaving me for dead.

"He took him."

There is not a shred of doubt in my mind that she knows exactly who I'm talking about. The mountain and the woods around us are a world of its own. As shifters, we've learned to live according to the laws of nature, only some of us decided that those laws valuing fairness and kindness would no longer be valid. Now, there are too many frightening unknowns. Even secluded here, protected by light magic, we're not completely safe. Time is ticking away.

"Oh my God," she presses her hand to her lips. "This is all my fault."

"No, you can't blame yourself," I tell her.

That is the last thing I want her to feel: responsibility for my state. Whatever happened was bound to happen, with or without her. It is simply how fate works. I believe she was destined to be here, and Vlad and I were destined to meet her. Everything else that has arisen from it is merely an obstacle that needs to be traversed. As it will be.

"I can and I will," she responds stubbornly. "If I didn't come here, I wouldn't have brought Kaige's wrath upon you. I should have just kept on going, anywhere but here."

The thought of her wandering the world alone, without anyone to help her makes me both angry and sad at the same time, a combination of emotions I'm not used to. I feel tenderness towards her, just like I felt for Xena. Only, Cat is so different from Xena, who would just wait for others to tell her what to do, to help her choose her way. Cat, on the other hand, had no such problems. She made her own decisions, and in case they were the wrong ones, she relied on herself to solve those problems. She refused help even when she needed it. In a way, she is Xena's complete opposite, and only now do I realize that Xena and I probably never would have worked out as a couple.

I don't want a child to take care of. I want a woman who knows what she wants, who is not afraid to make a mistake, and who will be brave enough to face hardship, alone or together with someone. Cat is that woman. But, the memory of Xena's love is still holding me back, even if it is merely a memory. One can become a prisoner of memory, of the past so easily that one doesn't even become aware of it until it is too late.

"You couldn't have foreseen any of this, so there's no point flagellating yourself for something that was completely out of your hands."

"But, why didn't he come for me?" she suddenly wonders, and it is this question that I was afraid she would ask. Of course, she is clever enough to ask the right questions. "Wouldn't it have been easier not to warn me, but just grab me while the three of us were out picking mushrooms together?"

I wonder if I should tell her. Taarus has instructed me not to, but I feel she has the right to know. After all, this is all about her, all because of her. Despite that, she is not to be blamed for any of this, and none of us consider her to be at fault. But, knowing her, if I tell her what's going on, she will rush in there like a fool, trying to save Vlad... provided he is still alive.

The thought of him being at the mercy of someone like Kaige enrages me, although there is little I can do in this bedridden condition. However, that doesn't mean that my rage is any less profound. Kaige has taken my brother, and one way or another, he will be forced to pay the price for that mistake.

Now, he wants to take Cat as well. I can't let that happen. Yet, I don't feel like it is my fight. Kaige is Cat's enemy. She is his own blood, and as such, she has the right to challenge him, without anyone objecting to it. I can do no such thing. I am merely a newcomer; I don't belong to their pack. He would merely scorn me and refuse my challenge.

This is Cat's fight. She needs to come to terms with her own past, and either kill Kaige or let him live. That is a decision only she can make. No one can make it for her. Consequently, it will be the decision that will reveal the path of the rest of her life.

"Because, you are not the only thing he is after," I finally decide to tell her everything.

Taarus won't like it, but aren't we all a clan? Shouldn't we all be open and honest with each other? Cat deserves to know everything, and together, we shall come up with a plan. I will help her any way I can, although in this physical condition, I am not much of an aid. Still, my mind is alert as ever, and perhaps, she could use it to her advantage.

"What do you mean?" she eyes me suspiciously. "It's me he wants and me alone. He regrets letting me go, because I am the only one who shares his blood, and as such, I am the only one who can challenge him for the leadership."

"That is all true," I nod, not surprised that she is well versed in the way a pack hierarchy functions. "But, Kaige is too confident to even consider the possibility of you defeating him. He is hiding behind that excuse."

"So, what is the real reason behind him almost killing you and kidnapping Vlad?"

"He is blackmailing you into doing exactly what he wants you to do," I say. "Here."

I reach towards the small table near the bed and grab a piece of paper from it. It was once folded neatly, but now it's crumpled and dirty. I'm still wondering whether I shouldn't have showed it to her, but now it's too late to change the path we've embarked upon. I convince myself that it will all end well, as long as she trusts her own wolf, her own instincts. Her wolf will know what to do.

"Read this," I instruct.

She grabs the paper from my hands, and I know the text by heart. I've read it more times than I can count, although before beating me to a bloody pulp, Kaige did mention why he was doing this.

This is for Ecaterina.

Unless you want Vlad to suffer the same fate as his brother, come and bring the book. You have until the full moon. I will be waiting.

Kaige

She lifts her gaze to mine, her lower lip trembling. She seems ethereal, effervescent, like a forest nymph from ancient tales I used to hear about as a child. They have always hidden themselves from both humans and shifters, because they are fearful of us. Now, I know why. It is shifters like Kaige who give the rest of us a bad name.

"How does he know the book is here?" She goes pale.

I shrug. "Almost everyone who's ever been inside these walls knows that. Once they leave the premises, you can't really control what they do or who they talk to. And, knowing where the book of Thoth is counts for a very interesting topic."

She tries to smile, but it's a weak effort. She is trying to wrap her mind around Kaige's plan, but it is all very simple. He wants the book, so he can cast evil spells and conquer all the clans and packs, pronouncing himself the ultimate pack leader. He is not the first one with such grand plans. He's not very original either.

"But... he can't have the book of Thoth," she gasps a truth that we are all aware of.

"I know," I assure her.

I use all my physical effort to lean over to her and take her by the hand, just like she took me the moment she entered. Her hand is cold, clammy. I press my thumb to the inside of her arm to feel her pulse. It's racing.

"You don't know Kaige," she continues. "You've all heard of his cruelty, but you haven't witnessed it firsthand. If he gets hold of the book of Thoth, there is no telling what horrible things he might do. I dread to even think about it."

"Taarus didn't want me to tell you about the message," I admit.

"That's probably because he knows I only need this one invitation," she replies.

"You can't possibly consider facing Kaige on your own."

"I'm not on my own," she says, her eyes burning with the fire I've only seen once in her. "I have seen my wolf. She will be my guide. She will protect me."

"Your wolf is the most beautiful thing I've ever seen," I tell her, and her jaw drops.

"You've seen her?" Her voice is barely audible.

"Of course," I nod. "That night when we – "

"Oh, my goodness! That happened!?" She lowers her head and buries her face in her hands. "I actually slept with you, both of you!?"

I don't know whether to frown or to laugh hysterically. Obviously, she believes that the whole thing was just a figment of her imagination, just a prolongation of her vision. While in fact, her vision ended way before she came to us in the library.

A part of me doesn't even want to burst her bubble, but I don't want her to think that night never happened. Because, it did. And, it meant more to Vlad and me than she must think.

"There wasn't much sleeping involved, but if you wish to refer to it that way," I know I'm mirroring Vlad now, but the urge is stronger than me. Still, she doesn't smile. She seems shocked. "Do you regret it?"

She pins me with her eyes. I know what my reply would be. Vlad has also shared with me his. But, I don't know hers.

"It was totally unlike me," she says, cleverly avoiding to actually answer the question. "I've never done anything like that before."

"I wouldn't care if that was all you did before," I explain, and she's a bit taken aback by my comment. Still, that doesn't make it any less true. "What I care is that you did it with us. I saw your wolf. I felt the way she marked me."

"You felt that?" she gasps once more. "When she put her paw on…"

"Yes," I smile. "Believe me, I felt it. I felt everything that night, and I still feel it. Don't pull away from something just because it is new or different from what you're used to."

"I… you're right," she nods. "When I relinquished control and just followed her, I felt so liberated. I felt like a new person, and yet, at the same time, I felt like myself, like my real self."

"That is what it feels to know your wolf," I agree. "That is the whole purpose of the visions. Especially for you who haven't shifted for the first time yet. You and your wolf sense each other now, so it will be easier to connect when the time comes. Just let her find you, and she will do the rest."

"I trust her."

"You have to," I remind her. "Otherwise, she will tear you limb to limb."

"Then, this means I have to go and meet Kaige," she tells me gravely.

"What?" I frown. "I never insinuated that."

"You didn't have to. I know what I need to do."

"No, Cat, you don't understand… it's a trap. They will be waiting for you."

"And, they don't know who they will be welcoming," she says with a wicked glimmer in her eyes. "I feel like this is why she's woken up. She wants to guide me there. She wants to be the tool to my vengeance."

"No, vengeance will only get you killed!"

I try to talk some sense into her, but I see now that Taarus was right. He didn't urge me to keep this a secret because he was afraid she would be scared, and she'd feel responsible. He urged me to keep it a secret so she wouldn't do a stupid thing like go there on her own and try to be a hero.

"Wait for Taarus to tell us what to do," I continue, hoping that she's reconsidering her plan of action.

"Vlad doesn't have that much time," she tells me something I myself know well. "You know Kaige won't keep him alive for much longer. We can't wait."

"Then, I'm coming with you," I try to get up from the bed, but the pain is overwhelming.

"You're injured," she reminds me. "You have to heal."

"But, you can't go alone." I can't let her do this. Then, both her and Vlad's blood will be on my hands.

"I will not be alone," she reminds me. "I will shift for the first time, and I will exact my vengeance upon the man who took my father's life."

I can see there is no way for me to change her mind. She will go with my blessing, or without it. I sigh heavily, as I my chest rises and falls with rapid breaths. She is much more stubborn than I thought she was. Much, much more.

"When you shift, completely let go," I advise. "Do not doubt her for a second, for she will sense it. Completely let her take over and she will know what to do."

"OK," Cat nods, armed with a new sense of purpose.

A dangerous purpose, one that could cost her not only her life, but the life of everyone here.

Chapter 22
Vlad

I'm desperately trying to untie my hands, but it's impossible. Someone's a pro at these knots. The sack over my head was unnecessary, and now it's making it harder for me to breathe. But, that's still not as concerning as what happened to Stefan.

The bastards caught us off guard, outnumbering us ten to two. If we were ready, we would have been able to take them down easily, but Kaige was even better prepared than we were. He knew exactly when to strike and how, so he could take us both out.

The last thing I remember seeing, before they pulled this damn thing over my head, was Stefan on the ground, blood oozing from him. I know why they didn't take both of us. Firstly, they only need one as bait. Secondly, they couldn't handle us both. So, they made sure that Stefan wouldn't get up.

He looked lifeless, but I know he's alive. I just know it. I feel it in my bones, the way I feel my wolf rattling the cage inside of me, beginning to be released, so he could take care of these assholes. Only, I can't do shit when I'm tied up like this.

Unexpectedly, I hear footsteps. They're getting closer and closer. I inhale deeply, and I recognize the stench. Before I can say anything, a hand pulls the sack off my face.

I'm in a small room. The walls are wooden. A shack, maybe or a cabin? I instinctively look for the door and windows. One door to my right, guarded by two thugs. The windows are boarded up. It would take too much time trying to break through them. So, the only way out is probably the same way I got in: the door.

A shadow stirs in the corner. It gets up, dragging a chair with its hand, resting it right in front of me. Then, he sits down.

"Kaige," I spit.

"Vlad," he grins at me. "Long time no see."

"Not long enough."

"Ah, I see the sting of old betrayal never ceases to hurt."

"Depends which side you're on," I remind him.

Stefan and I knew him a long time ago, when Kaige was merely a psychopath for sport. Now, he's a psychopath aiming to become the leader of the world or something.

"What the fuck do you want from me?" I watch his red-rimmed beady eyes and I feel like I'm facing a rat.

"Always eager to get the job done, huh?"

"That's Stefan, you asshole," I frown. "I like to take my sweet time, which is exactly what I'll be doing the moment I get out of these ropes and start pulverizing you into the dirt."

I stir on the chair a little, unable to sit peacefully and promise such things.

"Maybe I really did leave the wrong one alive," he pats himself on the chin, as if he's lost in deep thought.

I snort. "Stefan isn't dead."

"I'm pretty sure he was when we left him," he tries to convince me of something I know is not true.

He's leaning over to me, and I can't take my eyes off of his protruding brow bone and angular cheekbones, making him resemble a remnant from the neanderthal age.

"That just shows how much you know, you monkey," I reply. "Now, how's about you let me out of these ropes so we can settle this like men?"

"No can do," he clicks his lips, then shakes his head, his dark charcoal eyes focused on me, as if trying to pierce right through me. "You can't challenge me. You know the rules."

"Oh, and kidnapping others is obeying the rules? Go fuck yourself."

"You know, you're lucky Ecaterina wants you alive. Otherwise, you'd be dead, just like your brother."

I rattle the chair with the sheer strength of my tied-up body, just like my wolf is rattling my insides. It's ready to come out and do some damage. But, I feel it's still not the right moment.

"You say that about my brother one more time, and I'll – "

"You'll what?" he interrupts me. "Kick my ass? Hardly."

"What do you want with Cat?" I suddenly remember him mentioning her. "I swear, if you touch a single hair on her body, I'll – "

"There he goes again with the empty threats," Kaige snickers, raking his fingers through his jet-black hair.

He's definitely grown since the last time I saw him. He used to be a scrawny looking feller, and now, he looks like someone chiseled him out of the Malefic Mountains themselves. His muscles are visible through his clothes, and I bet he packs a mean punch. When I fight him, I'll need to be careful. Kaige always plays dirty. That's at least one thing that hasn't changed. That and his total insanity.

"But, alright, I'll satisfy your curiosity," he smiles.

Yet another thing which never seems to change. Bad guys always love explaining their plan to the helpless good guy. So, I'm all ears, because it might come back to bite him in the ass.

"I've always suspected that Ecaterina is the silver white," he starts. "You know, from the mythical silver whites clan? The ones that have gone extinct ages ago? Well, legend has it that the genes didn't disappear. They just got watered down, and eventually, the silver white will appear again."

"So?" I shrug indifferently. "You know that means that she will kick your ass once she transforms. There's no way you can beat a silver white in combat."

"I don't have to," he shakes his head. "I just want the book."

"The book of Thoth?"

Now, it's all starting to make sense. He found out Taarus had it. He knew none of us would willingly give it to him, so the only way he could get it was to blackmail someone into bringing it to him. Only, that's not gonna happen either.

"Well, sorry to disappoint you, buddy, but that plan is doomed to fail."

"Is that so?" He seems amused, but I doubt he knows much about Taarus. If he did, he'd know that there was no way in Hell Taarus would allow anyone to take the book outside of the confines of the Hermitage. Not for anything in the world.

"It is so," I nod. "Cat won't be bringing you the book for the very simple reason that she won't be allowed to take it anywhere."

"You seem to doubt her affections for you, or it just me?"

"Affections?" I frown.

How does he know all this? Then, it hits me. There is a fucking mole in the Hermitage. There was no other way he'd know all this.

"Affections or not," I decide not to deny any of it, "if she's coming, she'll be coming empty handed."

"We'll see about that," he snorts, but I can tell he's getting agitated, because every single thing I've told him makes total sense.

There's no way Taarus will let her take the book and bring it to this asshole. Now, if I could only loosen these ropes a bit, then I could show him who he's messing with.

"If you were any kind of a man, you'd fight me," I growl at him.

I want to piss him off, so he's angry enough to release me and fight me. That is my only chance of getting out of here.

"Or, are you too much of a chicken?" I add, just for flavor.

Unfortunately, he doesn't bite. Instead, he gets up, and pushes the chair away. It screeches against the stone cold floor, piercing through my ear drums. I groan silently at the displeasure.

"Your idiotic efforts at getting me to fight you won't work," he says.

Crap. He's seen right through me.

"What will get you to fight me?" I ask, out of any other ideas at this point.

"Nothing, so shut your trap," he hisses at me. "I gave her until the full moon, which is tonight. If she doesn't come, it will be easy to dispose of you, and also, quite a pleasure."

I don't say anything to that. I swallow heavily, feeling my throat drying. I try the ropes again, but they're so tight they're digging into my flesh. Maybe if I jump backwards and fall to my back, the chair might shatter. But, I can't do that with him and the thugs around. I need them gone for this.

"Yeah, yeah," I roll my eyes. "Are you done yapping? Cuz, I'm a bit tired here. And, if you aren't man enough to fight me, then just get the Hell out of here, will ya?"

He definitely wasn't expecting me to say something like that. His face turns red, and his lips part, probably to shout or screech, but he closes them immediately, shutting up like a clam.

"I'll make you eat those words when the time comes," he hisses again.

"Yeah, yeah," I shake my head, watching him leave the room. "Y'all come back now, ya hear?"

I chuckle to myself when he finally closes the door, leaving me with only one thug. He's standing by the door, his arms crossed at his chest. He looks pumped up, like a balloon. Those guys are usually just for show. They go down easily, so I'm not scared.

What I am worried about is Cat. What if that silly girl really decides to come over and try to rescue me? Stefan is hopefully back at the Hermitage by this point, and I'm sure Willow is treating him well. He should be back on his feet in no time.

As for me, I'm not worried. I've been in worse situations before. Even surrounded by more idiots like this one. I just need an opportunity, and I'll be out of these ropes.

Suddenly, I remember her. Cat's she wolf. The silver white. I remember being in awe of it when I laid my eyes on her. Such a mystical creature. I never thought I'd ever see one. No wonder Kaige wants her with the book. Her blood would make the spells in it twice as powerful. But, he would still need someone to read it. Taarus would never do it. He would rather die than allow the book to fall into the wrong hands.

There are so many things that might go wrong with this idiotic plan Kaige has concocted. Unfortunately, all of those things mean that people might die.

Stefan might die. Cat might die. The thought nestles like a cold wind inside of me, refusing to leave.

I can't let that happen. She is ours.

Chapter 23
Cat

When I leave Stefan's room, I know exactly what I need to do. I head straight for the library, trying to come up with a plan on the spot. What if someone catches me taking the book? Taarus or Willow? Will they let me go?

All logic assures me that there's no way that's happening. And, that makes sense. Taarus has been keeping it a well-guarded secret all this time. He can't allow it to leave the premises. Yet, I must have it. I must show it to Kaige, so he will fight me. I don't plan on giving it to him, but I doubt he would agree to fight me, unless I actually show it to him.

I open the door to the library slowly, like a thief in the night. Not only do I feel like that, but that is actually what I am. I am about to steal the most prized possession they have here at the Hermitage. I feel like shit, because they have welcomed me here with open arms, and by doing this, I am stabbing them in the back. Maybe, once this is all done, they will understand, and they might find it in their hearts to forgive me. But, for now, I can't let Kaige hurt Vlad.

I quickly scan the room. It's empty. I close the door behind me, and hastily head towards the bookshelf which is behind the armchair where Taarus usually sits. It only hits me now that I don't know where exactly the book rests when it's not in his hands.

I inhale deeply, closing my eyes. Maybe if I call out to my she wolf, she will come forth and help me find it. I try to drown out all noise inside my mind, focusing on just her. Nothing else. It's hard, because all I can think about is Stefan, all bloody and bruised, and Vlad, who is probably in an even worse shape.

Shhhh. I hear an inside voice try to calm me down.

I inhale deeply, then exhale. She is still nowhere to be seen. Frantically, I open my eyes. What if she has left me for good? What if she doesn't appear when I face Kaige?

Doubts are swarming inside my mind like poisoned arrows. I can't succumb to them. I need to have faith in my she wolf, like Stefan has urged me. She can't sense that I'm doubting her, because we won't be able to bond when I shift. And, that might be deadly for me.

I try again. Inhale. Then, exhale. There are no doubts. I am fully open to her. I give myself to her. I am her tool, and she is my guide.

I keep repeating these words like a mantra. However, she is still nowhere to be seen. I don't hear that familiar snarl, soft and tender and so strong at the same time. No matter how hard I try, I just can't seem to hear it.

Then, suddenly, the door opens. I smile. She's heard me. She's here.

I hear the sound of footsteps. I frown. It can't be her. She wouldn't be walking like that.

Quickly, I open my eyes and I see Taarus in front of me. Willow is still at the door, as if she's wondering if she should even get involved in this, or maybe just go back to the kitchen and let Taarus handle it. Luckily for me, she chooses to come in, then closes the door behind her.

"I see you've come for the book," Taarus states the obvious.

"I don't know where it is," I admit.

There is no point in lying. Not when he knows everything.

"Even if you did know, I couldn't let you take it."

"I know that," I sigh. "I don't plan on giving it to Kaige. I would never do that. I just need to show him that I have it on me, so he will agree to accept my challenge."

"My dear child," Taarus walks over to his armchair, his robe trailing after him like a dark snake. "The moment the book leaves the Hermitage is the moment we've lost it. Do you understand?"

"No..."

"It is protected here," he reminds me. "That is why Kaige can't just attack us and take the book himself. No matter what dark magic he might have on his side, it is still not powerful enough to take down the light magic protection that is still hovering over us."

"Can't we put the protection on the book while I take it out with me?" I plead.

"I'm afraid it doesn't work that way," he shakes his grey head at me.

I wonder what his wolf looks like. Is he one of the old greys? The wise old wolves who had paid the price of being too wise?

"The borders of the magic have been set a long time ago," he explains. "It's not just a matter of casting a spell on an object to keep it safe from harm."

"But, I can't leave Vlad..." My heart is heavy, laden with helplessness, the worst feeling of all. "You've seen what Kaige has done to Stefan. He almost killed him."

"Stefan and Vlad are well aware of the potential consequences," he comments. "And, sometimes, fate leaves emotions aside so it could make things right."

"How do I make things right?" I demand to know. "Stefan believes you. Everyone here believes you always know best. So, tell me then. What am I supposed to do? How do I save Vlad?"

Taarus doesn't speak immediately. I see I have left him speechless, but I'm not proud of it at all. I actually feel exactly the opposite of that. I want him to shout at me that I am wrong, and that he knows exactly what needs to be done. But, his eyes assure me that isn't so.

My heart sinks inside my chest.

"I will go even if it is without the book," I exclaim. "I will not sit here, while Vlad's life is hanging by a thread."

"Sometimes a life has to be lost in order for many others to be saved."

That is Taarus' reply. Just sit back, let Kaige kill Vlad and go on with your merry fucking lives. As if that would ever be possible for me.

My nostrils flare up angrily. I can't believe he is telling me to just let it go. Is the book really worth all the lives lost over it? I sure hope so.

"I refuse to believe that," I snarl at him.

Suddenly, there she is. Behind me. I feel her warm breath. She brushes her muzzle against my hand, leaving a moist stain. She has come to me. She wants me to know that I am on the right path, that I shouldn't stray.

I wont. I promise.

Now, I know that both Taarus and Willow can see my wolf. They are moving their eyes in the direction where she is moving. She is also not taking her eyes off of them.

"The silver white," Willow gasps, pressing her hand to her lips. "She is magnificent."

I lower my hand, raking through the wolf's soft fur. She is calm under my touch, just as I am calm under hers.

"I won't sacrifice him," I tell Taarus. "You can keep your book. I will go and save Vlad."

I turn to go, but Willow grabs me by the elbow. My she wolf growls loudly at her, and Willow immediately lets go. She is still overprotective of me. I guess that's a good thing. It sure will be when I face Kaige. It will be soon. Too soon.

I rub my wolf's fur once again, soothing her. Willow would never hurt me.

"Wait," Willow says, then she turns to Taarus. "What about the other book?"

I turn to him as well. "What other book?"

He pulls on his long grey beard, then massages his chin. It seems to help him think. He walks over to the bookshelf, and extracts two books, which were situated on the opposite sides of the shelf. I notice that they have the same kind of leather binding, the same kind of illegible writing.

"Are there two books?" I gasp.

"No," he replies. "One is the original. The other a mere copy I had made ages ago."

"I made him do it," Willow interferes. "Because I thought something like this might happen, and we would need a decoy book."

I smile. "Well, that solves everything, doesn't it?"

"Maybe," Taarus still doesn't seem convinced. "Those who have seen the book before can recognize it by its smell. You see, the copy we had made smells differently. I'm afraid that Kaige will recognize it's not the one."

"What if I stay far away from him?" I wonder. "Will he be able to tell then?"

"You'd have to be really far away," he voices his doubts.

"What if I just quickly pull it out of my backpack, then quickly shove it back in?"

"That might work," Willow jumps in. "Kaige won't pay much attention to it that way. He'll just see she's got a book, with the same binding, and he'll assume it's the one. Just like he'll assume that he has already won."

"Maybe," Taarus nods. "I just don't feel right sending you off on your own."

"That is the only way I want to do this," I remind him. "This man murdered my father."

"You know what I told you about revenge," he reminds me.

"This time, it's not only about revenge," I vow. "He has dared take yet another person I hold dear, threatening to hurt him. The other one he has already hurt. I can't stand idly by and let him think that he can get away with this."

"Just listen to your wolf," Taarus gives me the same advice. "Forget all about your human instincts, and just be her. Be a wolf."

"I'll try."

"There is no try, kid," Willow assures me. "You have only one chance."

"That is all I need," I smirk, taking the copy Taarus offers me.

I inspect it in my hands. It looks exactly like the original. Whoever has done it, did an amazing job. I'm sure Kaige won't know the difference, as long as I keep him occupied.

"And, don't worry, you won't need to convince him to fight you," Taarus suddenly adds. "I'm sure he already knows or has at least been suspecting that you are a silver white wolf. Your blood has magical properties, which can enhance the spells from the book."

"Really?"

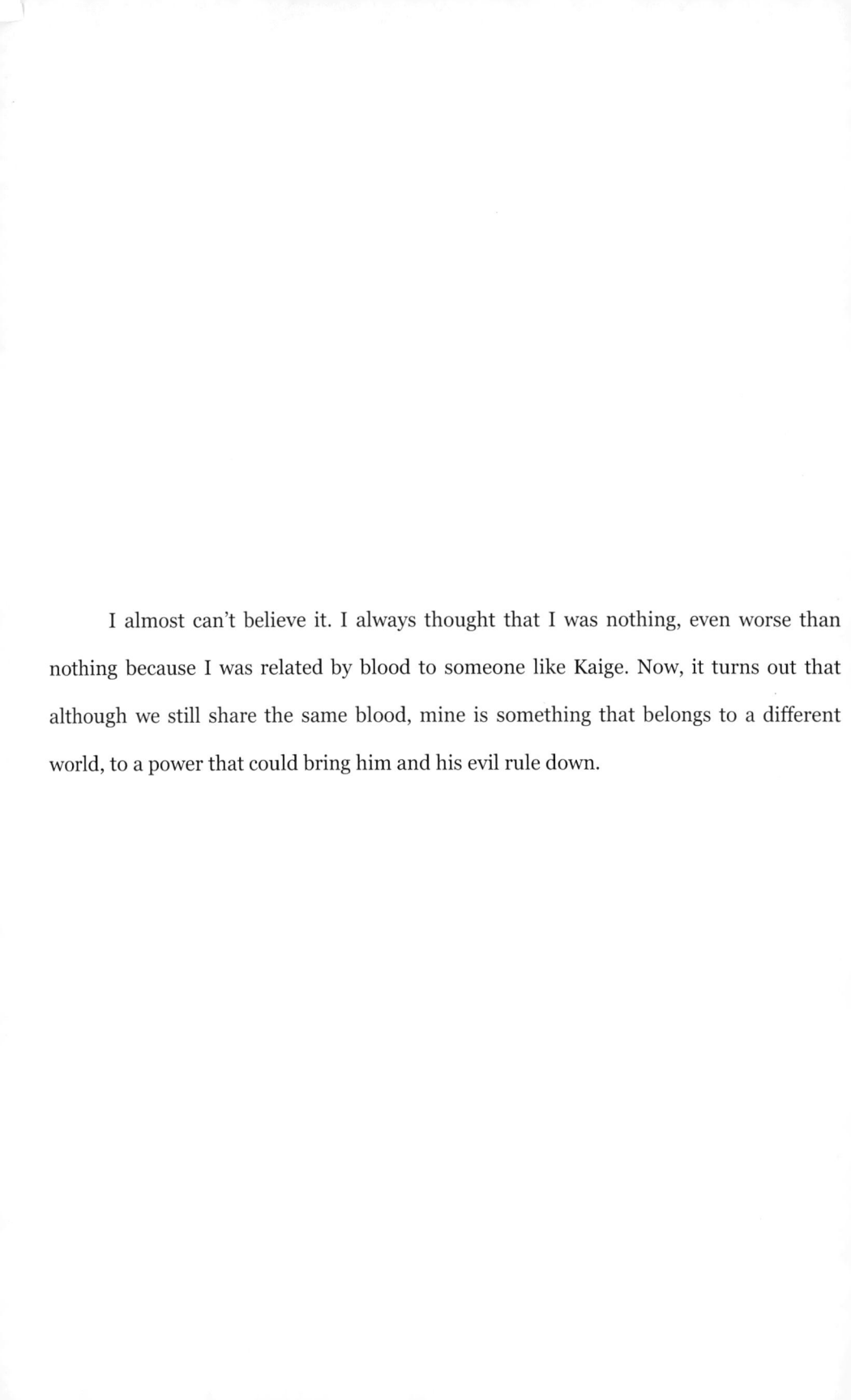

I almost can't believe it. I always thought that I was nothing, even worse than nothing because I was related by blood to someone like Kaige. Now, it turns out that although we still share the same blood, mine is something that belongs to a different world, to a power that could bring him and his evil rule down.

Chapter 24
Cat

I tread through the Wailing Woods, and it all feels like the first time, the time I was banished from my home. Only now, I am not running away. I am returning to the place of my roots, the place that very well might become my burial ground.

I try not to think so bleakly. The truth of the matter is that Kaige is dangerous. He's much more dangerous than I could ever imagine. He's never been an uncle to me, not in the real sense of the word. He's always been Kaige, the alpha, the same thing he was to everyone else.

The sun is already setting. I've been walking for hours. I have nothing but an inner compass which is, hopefully, leading me in the right direction. My backpack is hanging on my back, with the book safely tucked inside. A part of me still wonders if Kaige will see through the ruse. It's up to me to focus his attention on myself. An angry shifter is a careless shifter. As long as I make him see red, which shouldn't be hard, he will focus on me and not on examining the book.

I elbow my way through thick shrubbery, and I try to walk over small streams, not getting wet. Although that would be the least of my concerns. Strangely, I am not tired. I feel like I've been through so much these last couple of weeks, and especially these last few days. I've gotten to know myself more deeply than I ever thought possible.

My hidden desires have all surfaced, desires and needs I never even knew were there. Is this how it truly feels to be one with your wolf? I've only heard from others what this experience feels like, and I always wondered when it would be my time.

I thought, actually I hoped, my wolf would come to me as I watched my father lose his life. I can't help but wonder whether I could have done something. Maybe not, but at least I wouldn't be plagued by this gnawing feeling that I just stood by, doing nothing. My father died before my eyes. I was cast out, like a leper. They averted their gazes from me when my eyes met theirs. People I grew up with, people who were my friends, my family. I left that place with no one but myself, and I return there emboldened with a new sense of family, of belonging.

Somewhere on the distance, I see the faint flicker of fire. I am close. All the hairs on my body prick up. My she wolf is also here, by my side. She can sense them, too. Kaige's stench is overpowering. He's not alone. He is never alone. That is why it would be almost impossible to sneak up on him and take him by surprise.

With a heavy sigh, I realize that my best chance lies in me approaching him head on. I shall walk into the compound bravely, with my head held up high, stepping on the same ground that has drunk the blood of my father. I won't even blink. I won't show Kaige that I am afraid, although every inch of me is trembling. But, it's not only fear. It's a strange mixture of fear and exhilaration. I'm waiting for the moment when my wolf will take complete control.

Slowly, I come closer and closer, until I can already hear the crackling of the fire. There are distant voices, but I don't recognize any of them as either Vlad's or Kaige's. The rest I couldn't care less about. I linger for a moment, hidden by the deep shadows of the trees around me. The moment I take a step out, I will be in plain sight. So, I need to calm down and focus. I grip the straps of my backpack with my fingers. I inhale deeply. Then, I reveal myself.

Immediately, several eyes have spotted me. I pay no heed to them. They are of no interest or importance to me. I just need them to tell Kaige that he has called for me, and so, I am here. I keep walking boldly, my head held high. When he sees me for the first time since he has made me a fatherless child, I want him to see that he hasn't broken me. I am still standing strong. Stronger than ever.

My stride is confident, my chin aimed forward. Whispers flicker all around me. I hear them, but I pay no attention, just like I didn't on that fateful night. I walk all the way to the fire, in the middle of the compound, then I stop.

I look around. No one dares approach me. They are looking at me as if I were something abnormal, something they've never seen before. I don't know… maybe I am.

"I wasn't certain you would come," I hear Kaige's voice behind me.

I turn around slowly, completely in control of my entire body and the expression on my face.

"With such a lovely invitation, how could I refuse?"

He is staring at me from the other side of the blazing fire. The light is making his muscular, sharp jaw lines even more prominent. I notice there are a few fresh new cuts to his cheek. I can't help but smile, wishing it were me who made them.

He is wearing a bear skin on his back. Underneath, he is wrapped up in black cloth. I know what that means. With one effortless swoosh of his hands, he will be naked, free to shift on command. I look down at my own jeans and t-shirt, and I frown. I forgot to take that into account.

"Do you have it?" he asks, grinning at me.

I see his canines long and sharp. I bet if I were standing closer to him, I'd smell fresh blood on them. I doubt Kaige goes long without killing someone or something. It has become a pleasure to him.

He takes a step towards me, but I lift my hand to him. "Not so fast."

He smirks. His eyes hooded, stealing my breath. He had that same look in his eyes when he tore my father's neck open. I swallow heavily, feeling my knees turn to water. But, I manage to keep my balance somehow.

I need my wolf. Where is she? Did I lose her back in the Wailing Woods?

"Where is Vlad?" I demand, as my flesh tingles with both apprehension and excitement.

A soft snarl pricks my ears. There she is, and just like that, my fear transforms into anger. My every muscle tenses up, and my entire body locks up with rage. I need to calm myself down. I can't freeze. I have to flow like water. My movements need to be fluid, effortless. That is the only way I will be able to beat him.

Kaige lifts his hand. Immediately, Vlad is brought out from one of the shacks surrounding us. His eyes widen in alarm when he sees me. He tries to rush over to me, even with his hands bound behind his back, but the two guys by his side keep him steady.

"Cat!" he shouts my name. "Are you alright?"

"Ah, what a tender reunion," Kaige mocks us with a voice that makes my blood run cold. "But, I'm afraid we don't have time to kiss and make up. I've proven to you that Vlad is alive and well. I haven't killed him... yet. I've kept my end of the deal. Now it's your turn."

I slide my backpack down my shoulder. It falls to the ground. They're all watching. I can feel the heat of their gaze burning me with more intensity than the fire I'm standing right next to. I unzip the backpack and I take out a bundle wrapped in brown paper. A few gasps are heard.

I open the packaging and lift the book over the fire. The light bounces off the stained yellow paper. I'm far enough from Kaige. All he can see from here is the binding, which is identical to the original. His eyes sparkle with desire. His lips are parted, as he takes a step closer. I immediately take a step back, keeping the distance between us the same.

"Give it to me!" he demands.

"You're kidding, right?" I reply, as heat courses through my veins.

The she wolf snarls, electrifying me to the point of sizzling. I'm close. But, I can't shift now. Not yet. I need to speak to him a little longer. I need to push his buttons, to piss him off as much as I can.

Immediately upon saying that, I can see that his annoyance flares.

"Did you really expect me to just walk over to you and hand you the book?" I protest. "Are you really that stupid?"

It's only insult number one, and it's already working.

"I warn you, Ecaterina, it is not wise to call me stupid," he retorts. "Not when there is just one step separating Vlad from death. Do not tempt me to kill him."

"If you touch a hair on his body, I swear I will throw the book into the fire," I growl louder this time. I can hear the she wolf growling with me.

To my surprise, Kaige laughs loudly.

"Do you really think Taarus would allow that?" he continues. "I don't know how he let you take it outside the confines of the Hermitage, but I thank you for your resourcefulness. I suppose he is somewhere nearby, overseeing the whole thing, isn't he?"

I've never even considered that fact. Could it be true? Although I'm not carrying the original, Taarus really might be here.

"Come out, you old know-it-all!" Kaige shouts, but no one comes out.

"He's not here," I say. "It's only me."

"Then it's only you stupid enough to face me alone."

I smirk at his weak effort to insult me.

"I have brought the book just for you to see it, because you will never get your hands on it." I choose not to reply to his comment.

"Is that so?" He quivers with indignation. "You may not know it, but that is the only reason you and everyone at the Hermitage are still alive. If you hand me the book right this minute, I might consider leaving you alive, just so you can watch everyone around you die... just... like... your... father."

Rage pours right through me as he dares to mention my father.

"He was a better man than you'll ever be!" I snarl together with my wolf. She is as furious as I am.

Good.

"Good men die too soon," he snickers. "Haven't you noticed that?"

"And bad men live way too long, longer than they should have," I argue. "I've come to fix that. I challenge you, Kaige."

"And what if I refuse?" He stares me down mercilessly.

"You took my father's life. You were a brother to my mother. Your blood and my blood are the same. You cannot deny my right to challenge you."

"You are but a mere child," he scoffs. "You can't challenge the alpha."

"I can if no one here objects," I sneer, feeling the rage and need for vengeance fuel me. I turn to everyone around me, knowing they are all listening. "Does anyone here object to me challenging Kaige, your alpha?" I shout as loud as I can.

Fiery flames flicker all around me, but they are nothing compared to the flames of anger which are shooting through me. The wolf inside of me is desperate to come out. I can feel her trying to claw her way out. But, I can't show her until Kaige has officially accepted my challenge. I try to calm her down, but she doesn't want to be soothed. She wants to be let out to play, to hunt… to kill.

I wait a few more moments. My eyes traverse the sea of people around us. They all avert their gazes from mine. None of them dares look me in the eyes, even to refuse my request. The only reply I've received is silence, but that is enough of a response.

I focus my attention to Kaige.

"Your pack has spoken," I announce. "Or, should I say their fear and cowardice speak more than their words ever could. Now you have to accept my challenge."

He hesitates for a moment, then replies. "If you are so eager to die, then I shall gladly grant your wish, Ecaterina. I will enjoy burying my teeth into your scrawny neck, watching the life blood ooze right out of you. Then, I will kill Vlad, and everyone else at the Hermitage. And, there is nothing you can do about it."

I can only smile at him.

I feel it coming. She's here. And, she won't go away until I give her exactly what she wants.

Complete control.

Chapter 25
Cat

The time has come. Soon, I will shed my human self and transform into the self that I have always been meant to be. My wolf self. My true self.

I try to remember my father's words. *The first shift hurts the most. But, once you relinquish control to your wolf, it will be your guiding light. It will know what to do.*

His voice inside my mind is reassuring. It feels soothing. My heart aches at the sweet sound, and tears swell in my eyes. His words are comforting, but the truth in them is beyond terrifying. What if I get frightened, and my wolf senses it? She will tear me to pieces. It's no urban legend, as I used to think.

"Aargh," a moan escapes me.

The source of this discomfort is placed in the back of my neck, as if someone just pressed a scorching hot piece of coal to that spot. The painful sensation slithers down my back, like a river which separates into streams that only seem to infect the rest of my body, threatening to swallow me up whole.

I drop down to my knees, trying to focus on myself. I try to forget all about the fire burning bright in front of me. I try to forget all about the tall oak trees surrounding us. I try to forget about the cold, unforgiving earth underneath my feet. I try to forget about all the others around me. I am alone in this. Just me and my wolf. I have to trust in her, completely. Otherwise, I might not make it, and there will be nothing preventing Kaige from killing Vlad, just like he killed my father.

My father. He has told me about this so many times. He wanted me to be sure, to fully commit myself to this. Every detail has been etched into my memory. He's told me how it will feel. He's told me that I need to keep my eyes open and my breathing steady.

He's told me that the pain will be so great it will feel like I'm dying. In a way, it is a kind of a death. My human self needs to die so that my wolf self can be born.

I need to let go. My wolf will dominate me, then once she feels my fully committing to her, we will do this together. Only then will I be a complete being.

The pain in my neck is still there, intensifying. It cuts through me like a knife, a pain the likes of which I've never felt before. My head feels like it's about to explode. I try to keep my eyes open, but it's even worse. All I see are senseless colors of objects, places and people around me.

My skin itches first. I scratch my arms, my back, my neck, my legs. My nails leave red marks on my body. Something inside of me crackles.

My goodness. Are those bones breaking?

Another crack is heard, and I feel like someone stepped on my chest. I can't breathe. I'm suffocating. I lower my head to the ground, on my knees. I hiss angrily. I don't want to scream. It's bad enough that my first shift happens like this, in front of everyone, instead of in the safety and privacy of the Wailing Woods, like everyone else.

My skin stretches, my bones rearranging, cracking. I feel the coppery tang of blood in my mouth. Oh, God... it hurts like hell. How can I give into this when it hurts so much!?

My teeth crack, only to allow the appearance of fangs. Claws push out from underneath my nails. I'm still on my knees, but I feel I might lose consciousness at any moment. My body is in pain, but I know I don't want to die. Not like this. Not when there is still so much to do, most importantly kill this son of a bitch who is watching with perverse satisfaction the pain of my first shift.

Suddenly, there is a soft snarl inside my ear. She is urging me to stop fighting. So, I do.

The pain is still intent on tearing me apart. I feel like my insides are on fire, and not in a good way. It's like someone's poured molten hot lava down my throat, and now it's burning everything in its path. The moment I accept the pain and try to breathe through it, instead of away from it, it lessens barely noticeably.

Now, it's a tidal wave of pain, coming and going, and I have a few moments of peace between the onslaughts. Somewhere inside of me a little voice is telling me that it'll be alright. I just need to keep going.

I will survive this. I will become the wolf I was always meant to be. And, then I'm going to kill this son of a bitch with my bare claws and teeth.

I drop down to the ground, wasted. The new organism inside of me has taken over. When I open my eyes, it takes me a few moments to adjust to the blaze of the fire. I see it so much more brightly. I see colors I wasn't able to see before. The darkness has got nothing on me. I see further than ever before. I hear sounds I couldn't hear before, with my limited human hearing.

But, that's not the best part. I lift my head, feeling the ground on all fours. The feeling is strange, although not entirely unpleasant. I regain balance easily. My nose is high up in the air. I can smell it all. The woods around me. The fire. The shock. The sweat. The astonishment. The fear. They all ooze their emotions, and my wolf is able to pick up on them so easily.

When I look down, I see the silvery white fur of my big paws. I lift my muzzle. On the other side of the burning flames, Kaige has already transformed. He is much bigger than me, but he is a wolf just like any other. There is nothing special about him.

Me, on the other hand... I am unique. I am bold. I am brazen. And, I am here to kick ass.

He walks around the flickering flames, baring his teeth at me. He's not saying anything, although he can. Once in our wolf form, we are able to communicate telepathically. However, it seems there is nothing else either of us wishes to say.

I bare my teeth in reply. My fangs are shiny and new. I'm dying to try them out. I feel strength inside of me. My wolf is guiding me. It's a kind of energy that could never be described in mere words. A pure source of power.

He stands before me, a beast in his own right. He wants me to fear him, to revere him. I can't do any of those things. I snap my jaws at him, to show him that I'm not afraid. His hackles rise up, as he plants his paws firmly on the ground. He seems to be waiting, his ears shooting up at the sky.

Slowly, he starts circling me. I mirror his movements. We're both waiting for the other to make the first move. I thought at first that it would take me a while to get used to walking on all fours, but it comes so naturally, as if I've been doing it all my life.

I look at his stance. He might try to pounce on me, and I need to be ready. All I need is one opening, one mistake on his part, for me to win this fight and exact my revenge.

He growls at me, but I don't even blink. Everyone around us is silent, but I don't need them to be. It's become easy to drown out every other sound apart from Kaige's breathing. I can hear when it hastens. I can hear when it slows down.

All of a sudden, he charges, but I manage to evade his attack in the last minute. He skids through the dirt, immediately ready for another onslaught. I lower my front body, focusing on him. He lunges again, his mouth wide open and his pearly-white fangs glistening, sharper than knives. He's aiming for my throat, but I sacrifice my foot instead to his teeth.

He digs into my foot angrily, and it only takes me a second to open my mouth wide and grab him by the neck. He squeals, releasing me from his grip. I look at my paw. It's bleeding silvery red, but I feel no pain. I don't know how that's possible, but I don't question my wolf. She knows what she's doing.

My ears prick up at him. My temples throb with rage. I want him to attack me once more. But, he seems to be on the defense this time, biding his time. He's more careful. Blood trickles down his neck. He's hurt.

Good.

He snaps his teeth at me, snarling. But, he's lost his authority. He has only one way of gaining it back, and that is to defeat me. A mere child who dares defy him, who dares challenge him.

Unwilling to wait any longer, I throw myself at him, biting him on the head, on the neck, wherever my teeth land on his body. I'm attacking him with such fury, he's unable to fight back. I tear bits and bits of his fur, his flesh, until he is lying on the floor, in a pool of blood, with parts of his flesh scattered about him.

He is breathing heavily, his chest rising then lowering. It's the strangest, most satisfying déjà vu.

I walk over to him, looking at him from above. It would be so easy to kill him. All it would take is just one bite. Just one blow. And, he would be no more. But, my wolf doesn't want me to. She wants him to know the pain of living without anybody, the pain of being hated by the whole world. It's a fate worse than death.

"Don't worry," I tell him with the voice inside my mind, but I know everyone else can hear us. "I won't kill you. You don't deserve to die as a warrior. You deserve to be outcast like the piece of shit that you are."

He doesn't say anything to that. He doesn't need to.

The tongues around me are no longer caged. They are in disbelief that things can actually change. A wolf howls somewhere in the distance. I raise my head to the full moon. I howl loudly. Proudly.

All it takes is one brave soul to make a change.

Chapter 26
Cat

I lift my gaze. Everyone around me has shifted. I recognize scents, not faces any longer. I'm searching for a familiar scent, the one that drove me here. I'm barely paying any attention to the fact that everyone has turned against Kaige, and he is being forced out of the Wailing Woods. I don't know where he will go, but one thing's for sure. He will be the only one ever not to be admitted to the Hermitage if he seeks shelter there.

Leaves rustle somewhere nearby. My ears prick up. All my senses are still heightened to the brim. I look up and see his eyes. I'd recognize them among a million other men, a million other wolves. His scent is all I want, all I need. He brings his muzzle to mine, gesturing at me to follow him. Then, he disappears into the Wailing Woods.

I run after him, as we both catch a new scent, something completely unfamiliar. It takes a while to get there, but we eventually do. In the silent depths of the Wailing Woods, right in the middle of a clearing, washed by the moonlight, I see a deer. She's young, maybe not even two years old. I wonder what she is doing all alone.

I notice that Vlad has stopped as well. His instincts have kicked in, just like mine. It's not that we want to hunt this poor thing down. We need to. I want to turn away and just head back to the Hermitage, but I can't stop thinking about her thick neck and me digging my teeth into it.

I look around. There are numerous paths back into the woods where the deer might run away if we jump her now. Vlad approaches me so silently that not a single leaf underneath his paws stirs. The night is completely still. His steel blue eyes haven't shifted. They only seem more sparkly now.

I gaze at him in awe. He is magnificent, standing by my side. His fur is thick and luscious, dark grey with patches of chocolate brown. His claws are long and pointed. He's not thinking anything, yet I can hear his desire. It's easy to pick up on it, because it is exactly what I'm feeling, too.

He wants me. And, good heavens, I want him as well.

I inhale his scent, musky and masculine. He turns to me for a quick moment, nuzzling me softly with his muzzle. His touch is hot, burning me up. I want more. Yet, something's missing, and I know exactly what it is.

Better yet, who it is.

I moan against his closeness. The deer's head lifts up apprehensively. A moment later, she is but a mere memory and the clearing is devoid of any presence, save for our own.

My flesh tingles under his hot breath, and another surge of warmth spreads through me, as we circle each other. But, it's not like Kaige and I. No. That was a fight. This is something completely different. Everything about Vlad is masculine. His dominance is easy to sense. It's overpowering. I'm sure that he could have taken on Kaige himself in his wolf form. So, I wonder why he hadn't.

Then again, maybe things were meant to be this way. It's not a good thing to question fate. My dad once told me this. So, I won't. I'll consider myself damn lucky. He licks my nose. It almost tickles, but I don't chuckle. I couldn't even if I wanted to. Instead, I do the same to him.

Suddenly, we hear another branch crack somewhere close to us. Vlad pulls away immediately, but he remains close by. I don't need his protection, but it feels good to know that he's here in case I need him. We don't need any words between us. Instinct does it all for us.

I don't know what is approaching us, but my head is dizzy, and I can't focus on the potential approaching danger. I'm drunk on Vlad's scent. My wolf has fallen for his like crazy. I can't even explain it. It's just too primitive. Too raw. It feels even more liberating than that night the three of spent together.

Stefan... I need him here.

Another rustle is heard, closer this time. Vlad doesn't growl. He doesn't snarl. His gaze is focused on the direction where the noise is coming from. But, it doesn't seem like he is concerned. He seems to be merely waiting for something, or someone.

I push myself closer to him, rubbing myself against his fur. My entire body sizzles at the touch. I can't deny the attraction, the sheer and utter need I have for him. Yet, there's still something missing. I can't just let go and bond with him.

I hear the sound of leaves rustling. Finally, I see another head. Another set of eyes I could never mistake for anyone else's.

"Stefan!" my mind calls out to him, while my body is drawn to him instantly.

The three of us come together, and the closer we are, the more intense this yearning, this need becomes. I nuzzle Stefan, then Vlad. I see the devotion in their eyes.

"So beautiful," I hear Stefan's voice inside my mind.

His voice sounds hollow. It lacks that human element to it when he speaks, but I feel like this type of communication is more liberated. I can think whatever I wish, and I know that my thoughts will be conveyed simply and correctly. All restrictions have disappeared.

Vlad comes to my other side. I realize now why I'm so drawn to them both at the same time. I love Vlad for his charm, for the way he always knows what to say to make me feel better. I love Stefan for being my protector, for being strong when I had no strength left in me. For a moment, I wonder if they would want to fight over me, but that seems ludicrous. We all want the same thing. We want one another.

The intensity of my own emotions threatens to take over, not allowing me to think about anything else. I just feel... an everlasting need. Bathing in the soft glow of the moonlight, I know I am exactly where I need to be. I feel like myself with my wolf self, and with these two men who have accepted me as I am from the first moment they laid eyes on me.

Still, I can't believe I am here. I can't believe I am about to do this.

Right now, there is nothing more important than my most basic instincts which reveal my most inner desires. As I gaze into their eyes, I see the same kind of hunger, the same desires.

"I want you..." I think to myself, forgetting that everything I think is immediately transferred onto them.

They get even closer to me, this pull between us so raw and unapologetic.

"You are mine," Vlad tells me.

"Yours..." My mind is quick to reply.

"You are mine," Stefan repeats.

"Yours..." My thoughts are faster than my lips ever could be.

"Ours..." they murmur together, and all I can do is rub myself against them.

After our vows, the forest around us suddenly becomes quiet. I look up. The night sky looks like an explosion of a million tiny stars, all of which represent a single wish someone has made, just waiting to come true. I wonder if my own wish was waiting up there, only to be taken down on this very special night.

I belong. I finally belong. The thought swirls inside my mind, and I don't care if they hear me or not. I belong to them both and nothing in this world could have made me happier. My very soul has been bared in this communion, and I know they feel the same.

My wolf growls softly. All this feels so terrifying and thrilling at the same time. When you can't resist something, it is easy to give in to it. I rub against them, and their muzzles feel the softness of my silver white fur.

I thought claiming someone would be more aggressive, that it might even include shedding of blood, because you need to mark someone as yours, as belonging to you. But, this is completely unlike anything I had in mind. I never expected such tenderness, such loving care. I feel as if our souls have exited our bodies somehow, and they are hovering over us, amalgamating. It feels overpowering, the sensation taking everything out of me. It's unstoppable.

That same yearning pools underneath my tail. Instinctively, it points upward. My most primal instinct has taken over. All I want to be is taken. Claimed. Made theirs in every way possible, in any form we take. As humans, we are held back by what the human civilization has imposed upon us. As wolves, we are under no one's control, only our own wolf's.

Their teeth nip at my fur, at my ears. I hear them both call out my name, thick and heavy, like the air around us, filled to the brin with a sensation that we will eventually fully give into.

Suddenly, our three muzzles press together at the tips of our noses. Desire takes over. I lick Stefan's face. He tastes salty and sweet at the same time. Vlad nuzzles around me, then softly nibbles on my neck. I feel the sharpness of his teeth digging into my fur only for me to recognize the sensation. Never to hurt. Only to pin. Only to pleasure.

Suddenly, my fur starts to glisten. At first, I just think it's the reflection from the rays of the moonlight. It sparkles like someone spilled diamond dust all over me, brighter and brighter, until I'm burning like a candle in the darkness. Vlad and Stefan take a step back, mesmerized.

Something is happening. Something beyond my comprehension.

I fully let go. I feel myself being lifted off of the ground and my wolf lifts up her head and howls into the night.

So, this is what bonding feels like...

Chapter 27
Cat

I return to my human form much more easily than shifting to my wolf form. I listen to the sound of my breathing. It is the only thing I can hear, as my gaze falls on the two naked men before me. They look like statues, glistening under the light of the moon. Stefan is slightly more muscular, but Vlad doesn't lack anything in that respect.

As the first time, Vlad approaches me, his hand finding my cheek. His touch is scorching hot, as his brilliant blue gaze burrows into me. He presses his lips into mine possessively. I return the favor with equal passion. He leans me backwards, laying me down softly. The grass underneath me feels velvety supple, as it envelops my body.

I feel another pair of hands on my thighs, enticing me to open them. I close my eyes, as Vlad's mouth ravages mine. His tongue explores the depth of my hunger, knowing there's so much more of it hidden inside of me.

That very moment, I feel the warm flicker of Stefan's tongue on the most tenderly sensitive bundle of nerves between my thighs. My mind is a blank. All I can feel is the build up nestled in my lower abdomen.

I gasp at the sensation, as Stefan's tongue strokes over me slowly, tantalizingly. I gasp as Vlad pulls away only to allow me to breathe, then locks his lips to mine once more. I offer myself up to both of them, my body trembling, wanting more of this sweet torture.

I hear Stefan's murmur softly between my thighs, and I can't help but smile against Vlad's lips. Stefan suddenly sucks my pussy lips into his mouth and starts sucking. Inside of me, a new source of pleasure unfurls, revealing depths I never even thought were possible.

His skilled lips and tongue are only making my already desperate need even more needy. I writhe under their kisses, moaning softly. Stefan parts my folds, his tongue sliding into me effortlessly. I buck towards him, my fingers grabbing at his curls, pulling him closer to me. I never want him to stop.

Vlad's kisses are growing more intense by the minute. His hand finds my breast and starts playing with my pebbled nipple, pinching it, swirling it, teasing it. Stefan is driving me crazy, lapping at my very core, his finger rubbing on my swollen, wet clit with steady pressure which only seems to bring me to the edge. My senses are still heightened, and I simply lose control over myself. My very core explodes. My core clenches. Everything inside of me is fiery bliss. I grip at Stefan's hair, holding him between my thighs. That is where he needs to stay.

The sight of him is such a turn on, as his head bobs. Vlad's lips spill kisses on my neck tenderly, only enhancing the pleasure of my orgasm. My entire body trembles, as my pussy juices leak out of me. Stefan laps them up hungrily, his tongue still exploring my depths, following every spasm. He is as greedy for this as I am. All three of us are.

I never want him to move from there, but I know that feeling him inside of me will be even better. Suddenly, he withdraws his lips and his devilish tongue, only to help me onto my knees. There is something animalistic in the way they want to take me this time, and I don't mind. On the contrary, I want this as much as they do, if not even more.

He spreads my legs from behind, while Vlad kneels before me, his cock springing before me, like an offering. It's already beading with precum, and I lap the drops hungrily, feeling the tangy saltiness on my tongue.

"Oh, fuck..." Vlad groans, and his words have exactly the effect on me he's probably hoping they would. I'm so turned on I feel like I could dissolve any moment.

I'm on my knees before them, trembling, begging to be taken, to be made theirs now and again, forever more. The thought comes so naturally, so effortlessly. It is not only a thought. It is a truth. I never want anyone else ever again. I am forever marked, forever taken, forever theirs. And, that is exactly how I want it to be.

I open my mouth to welcome Vlad inside of me, hot and bulging. He palpitates in my mouth, as I take him all the way in, to the back of my throat. He moans again and again, grabbing a handful of my hair, but he doesn't push himself into me. He's letting me take the lead.

Stefan brushes against my painfully needly pussy lips. I'm dripping wet. I'm so desperate to be fucked that it is at the same time an embarrassment and a frenzied craving.

"What do you want me to do to you?" I suddenly hear Stefan say, and my mind explodes. I feel his finger inside of me, wet and hot, stretching me. He immediately adds another finger, and the sensation becomes just a little bit painful as my body adjusts to the new feeling. "You have to tell me, otherwise I will stop."

"Don't stop..." I pull away from Vlad's cock to plead. "I don't want you to ever stop... neither of you..."

Stefan adds another finger, and now the sensation is unbearably pleasurable. I buck against him, wanting more.

"Tell me what you want," Stefan demands in a voice that makes my pussy throb just hearing him speak. "What should I do to you?"

"I want you to fuck me until I can't breathe... I want you to make me cum all over your throbbing cock inside of me... I want Vlad to explode in my mouth and make me swallow every single drop of his cum..."

I have no idea where all that came from, but once I started speaking, I couldn't stop until it was all out of me.

Stefan leans over to my ear and whispers. "Good girl."

I feel his hands spread my ass cheeks, the tip of his cock pressing against my entrance. He separated my slick, wet folds easily, then slides in forcefully. I open my mouth, moaning, and Vlad's cock presses against my lips. I allow it entrance, sucking it, licking, teasing it with my tongue. His cock has become engorged, even bigger and thicker than the previous time I took it into my mouth. It almost doesn't fit. My jaw protests, but there is nothing else I can do but keep sucking and kissing and licking.

I open my eyes, admiring his smooth skin, glistening in the moonlight. Stefan is fucking me faster now, his body in perfect alignment with mine, as if they were made perfectly for each other. There is no more ache. My pussy has fully adjusted to his length and thickness, and all I can feel is getting closer and closer to the edge once again. I can't believe I'm about to cum again so quickly after the first time. What are these guys doing to me? They are driving me crazy in more ways than one, that's for sure.

Stefan's cock slides into my passage, taking my breath away with each thrust. We sigh loudly, moaning and groaning.

"Oh, fuck Cat... you feel so tight..." Stefan murmurs, and his words throw me over the edge.

I thrust backward, allowing him into me deeper, more fully. His fingers dig into my hips, pulling me closer to him. My body convulses, trembling with intense pleasure that washes over me once more. He keeps pumping his powerful cock into me, stiffening just a moment after me, thrusting a few more times, then withdrawing. I feel a gaping hole inside of me now, without him there, as our juices leak out of me mixed together.

Still quivering, I focus on Vlad now. My hand grabs his balls, and I start fondling them, as the tip of his cock slides down my throat, deeper than ever. I hear his guttural groan, and I know he's close. All it takes is a few more thrusts into the moist wetness of my mouth, and I feel his hot thick cum explode inside of me. I swallow every bit of it, savoring the tangy taste.

Within seconds, all three of us flop to the side, breathing heavily.

I look up at the sky. The night is dark, but the moon is bright, and it almost feels like daytime. The stars are scattered in the sky. I lift my finger, pinpointing as many as I can, drawing lines between them. I have no idea why I'm doing it, but it calms down my frantic breathing.

When I turn to the side, Stefan's eyes are already closed. To my right, Vlad is gazing at me lovingly. He smiles when our eyes meet. I smile back.

I feel wonderfully drained of every shred of energy that I had. Now, I need to be refilled. My heart pounds like crazy, my lips still swollen and slightly sore. But, I love it.

I love everything about my new life, and with that wonderful thought I close my eyes and drift off to sleep.

Chapter 28
    Cat

It's been a whole day since the events that seemed to clear my past and allow me entrance into a whole new chapter of my life, one I am still learning new things about. I think I slept almost 24 hours, and it feels great waking up in the same room of the Hermitage. Although I'm still not certain what my next move will be, this place still awakens tenderness inside of me. Perhaps staying here won't be such a bad thing after all. But, is it my fate to stay?

I stretch my arms high up into the air and walk over to the window. I open it, and let the fresh breeze hit my nostrils. The fragrances of the mountain and the woods around us are all intertwining in the air, and I can sense every single element of it. The moss. The dirt. The leaves. The grass. The water. Everything.

I listen for that soft snarl in the back of my head, but I can't hear it. Still, I smile. I know that she's in there. She is me and I am her. There is no doubt about it. We have become one.

In all honesty, I don't remember how Stefan, Vlad and I got back to the Hermitage that night. After we were done... well, bonding, let's say, it's all a blank, until I woke up this morning. A part of me thinks it's all just some crazy dream. Maybe it's all the result of Willow's potion, and I'm still under its spell, even after all this time. Only, I know better.

This is reality. I fought Kaige and I won. I have avenged my father's death. I don't know if he would be happy with that fact or not, that I risked my own life willingly, when he lost his trying to save me. All I can say is I hope that he is proud of me.

About half an hour later, I find myself knocking on the door to Taarus' room. The copy of the book of Thoth is in my hands. That is yet another mystery I can't explain. When I woke up, I found my backpack nestled safely by my bedside. So, whoever brought me back home, made sure that the copy also returned with me.

A few moments later, the door opens and Taarus smiles at me.

"Welcome back," he says, as if he didn't know whether or not I returned, until now.

He moves to the side to let me in. I walk inside, and hear the door close behind me. He is alone. I was sort of hoping that I'd find Willow here as well. It's easier to tell the whole story of what happened once, when they're both here. Oh well. I guess I'll have to keep repeating it. Maybe some stories are worth being told over and over again. I smile at the thought.

"This is yours," I say, taking out the copy of the book and handing it over to him.

He takes it, with a smirk. "I take it that it has served you well, then."

"Kaige barely paid any attention to it."

"How come?" Taarus wonders.

"I pissed him off first," I chuckle.

He smiles. "That was a good strategy."

He walks over to the bookshelf and places the book that has saved us all back in its rightful place. I guess in a way, this book is as important as the original, because it has served an even greater purpose. It has allowed us to get rid of an oppressor. Now, my clan is free. We are all free.

"So, now what?" He suddenly turns to me.

His dark eyes are staring at me. I feel like he already knows the answer to all the questions he might ever ask. His wrinkles must stand for every hardship the wolf clans have ever gone through, and I could keep counting them for days. His entire countenance is that of an old sage who has been here on earth since the first day of its creation. As such an omnipotent being, his role is clear. It is not to guide us. On the contrary, he is only here to listen, to help us reach a solution to a certain problem, but he is distinctly forbidden from interfering.

"I don't know," I shrug, looking around, then walking over to a chair that didn't seem particularly comfortable, but I still felt the need to sit down.

"What is your wolf telling you?" he wonders.

"I haven't asked her," I reply a little nervously, half joking.

"Some questions don't need to be asked. You either already know the answer or you will never know it. Which one are you?"

"I don't know what I am, to be honest," I sigh. "I'm different from all the other wolves. I know Stefan and Vlad have made me their mate, and I couldn't be happier about it, but who else will accept me so different, so strikingly dissimilar and maybe even dangerous, if I lose control?"

"Are you afraid that you might lose control and hurt someone?" he continues with his incessant questions, but somehow, I don't seem to mind.

I know he only wants to find out what's in my heart and help me realize the truth of my condition. Only then will I be able to decide on what my next step should be: should I stay or should I go.

"I trust my wolf," I reply without a shred of a doubt.

"As you should," he nods, his long beard touching his lap, Then, he leans back into the armchair, tilting his head a little. "So, what are you afraid of then?"

"I'm not afraid."

"You seem afraid," he shrugs. "I'm only telling you what it looks like from someone else's perspective. If it's not fear, what is it then?"

"I'm... worried..." I struggle to find the right word that's not fear. "I'm worried that being different means I have no place here."

"Why on earth would you be concerned about that?" he chuckles for the first time in ages.

His laughter is melodious, although his voice seems to be centuries old. But, it sounds like a soft waterfall which lulls you to sleep.

"I don't know," I admit. "Different is always... shunned."

"But, you know what the Hermitage stands for," he reminds me.

"I do..."

"You know, I believed you would find out on your own," he tells me. "Especially knowing how connected you are to the book of Thoth."

"You mean the blood?"

"Not only the blood," he shakes his head at me. "Everything."

"What do you mean everything?" I frown.

Even after all this time, it seems that Taarus has kept some parts of our story a mystery.

"The silver whites are protectors of the book of Thoth," he finally reveals. "The guardians. It is in your blood. You are intricately intertwined. However, you shouldn't feel obliged to this role. Your blood isn't pure silver white blood. It has been watered down, but that doesn't make it any less powerful. Still, the role would require you to stay here and... well, basically do what me and Willow have been doing for decades."

"Stay here, keep the book and the Hermitage safe?" This is what it boils down to.

"Yes," he nods solemnly. "It is a serious responsibility. Thousands of outcast wolf shifters count on this place. It has been a home to many until now, but it will continue to become a shelter for many more. This means that it must stay alive. It must keep its doors open, and its walls must stay protected by the light magic."

I stop to think about it. I always believed I would eventually leave this place, after becoming strong enough to defeat Kaige. It has become my focus in life. In fact, it has become everything my life revolved around until this point. Now that I find myself free from the shackles of the past and having bonded with two other wolves who have become my mates, I know I can't make any decisions without involving them.

"If I stay here, then Stefan and Vlad must stay with me," I'm thinking out loud. "Because we have – "

"Bonded," he finishes my thought. "Yes. I know."

"How do you know?"

It's not something other wolf shifters can sense. They can only find out if they've seen it or if they were told.

"I was with Stefan when he heard the call," he explains. "He was in bed, but suddenly, he got up. He walked over to the window and heard your howl."

I only remember the howl. I wasn't even sure what it meant at the time. However, it's obvious that my she wolf knew exactly what she was doing. She was calling out to him, to come get me.

"I witnessed his shift right in his room," Taarus continues. "Then, he jumped out of the window and went after you."

I blush at the thought that Taarus knows what's happened. He notices, and smiles.

"Don't worry," he says gently. "I may be old, but not that old not to remember what it is like to bond with someone, and to have that connection."

"Have you bonded, too?" I ask, but immediately bite my tongue. "I'm sorry. I didn't mean to pry." I look down at my feet, a little embarrassed. It isn't my place to ask such questions, although I feel like we've grown closer in the last several days.

"It's quite alright," he assures me. "It was such a long time ago, but I still remember it as if it happened yesterday. She was a member of the opposing clan. They were our rivals. She was the daughter of the chieftain, and our two fathers hated each other's guts. As you can imagine, our love was forbidden. It was unthinkable, and yet, it happened. We took each other's innocence even before we shifted."

He pauses, and I know why. What he and that girl did goes against every ancient law imaginable. Sleeping with someone before your first shift means that you have tainted yourself and that other person for your true mates. Because, you can only recognize your true mate in your wolf form. Your real form.

Luckily, the laws have eased up in the last few decades, so such transgressions are frowned upon, but they wouldn't cause much uproar. At least, not like they would have in the past. If you slept with someone before your first shift, you would simply need to bond with that someone in your wolf form, and problem solved. Whether or not that person is your true soul mate or not... that is your problem to deal with later on.

"So, they banned us, and tragically, she died giving birth to our first and only child." His voice has grown softer, saddened by the burden he has just shared. Such loss is something one never gets over.

"Is your child here?" I wonder.

Seeing I'm prying already, why not ask even more questions? It only makes Taarus seem like less of an old sage and more like a real man made of flesh and blood, and maybe just a little bit of old magic.

"No," he shakes his head. "He has found his destiny elsewhere. And, I'm happy it is so."

"Your destiny seems to be here, though," I tell him, but I'm sure he already knows this.

He smiles. "Yes. What about yours?"

Maybe he's right. Maybe I should just let go of any farfetched ideas I have of a future that might not even be for me. This is where I have found my new home. Should I really leave it, just because my feet itch to see the road?

"I think... I'd like to stay," I hear myself say.

The wolf snarls softly into my ear.

I smile. She likes the idea. She wants to stay here, too. After all, this is as much her decision as it is mine, now that we are one. I feel her with me all the time now. Electrifying and fulfilling. Her presence is pure energy. I tremble at the thought that this is me now. This beautiful, mesmerizing creature who is brave and relentless, who will not back down before anyone ever again.

"If that is your wish, then it will be our honor to have you," Taarus bows his head to me. Then, he lifts it back up and looks deep into my eyes, into my very soul. "With every choice, some paths close while others open. With this choice you have made for yourself, and for us as well, you have shifted and changed the future. I look forward to see where these new paths will lead us."

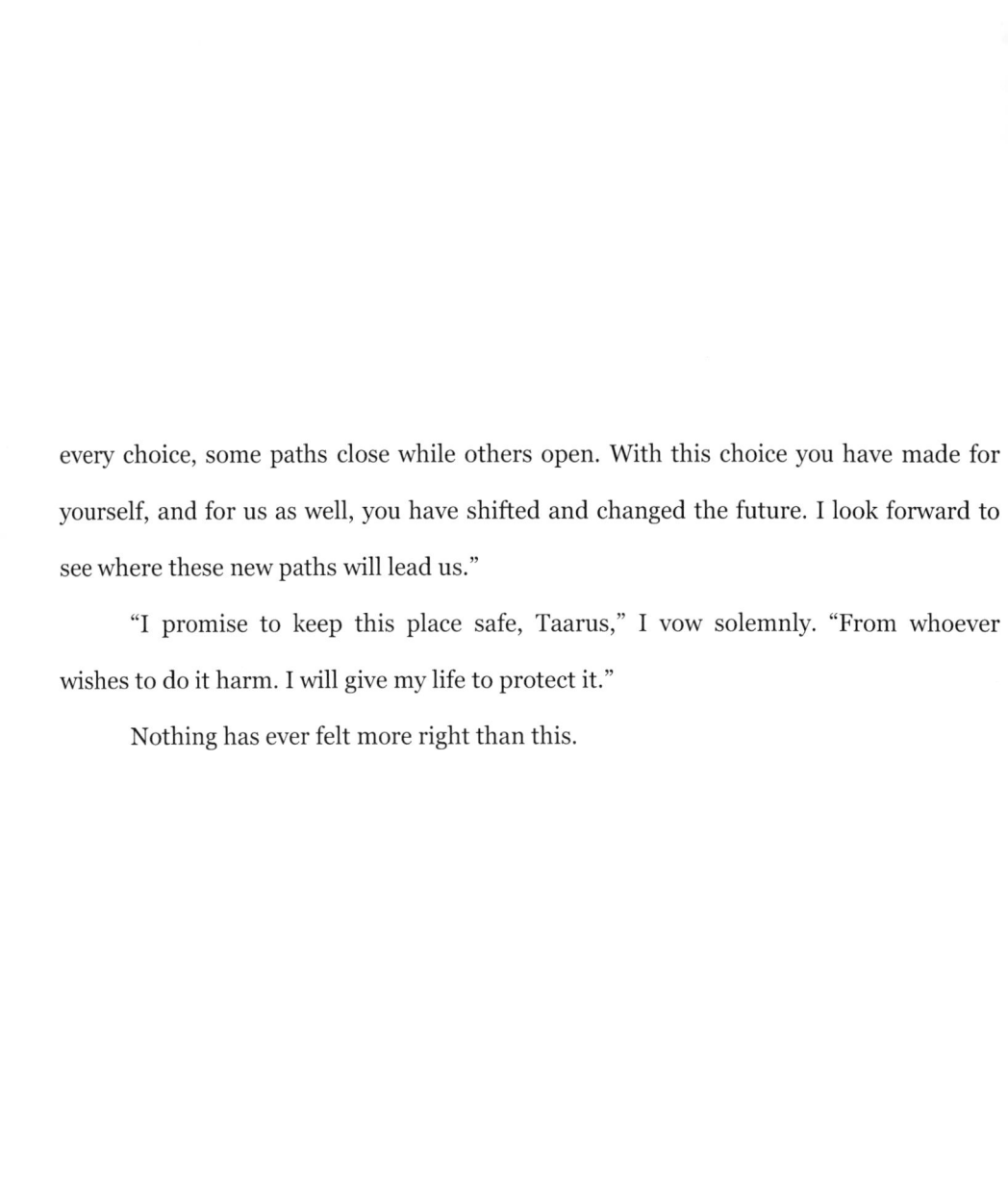

"I promise to keep this place safe, Taarus," I vow solemnly. "From whoever wishes to do it harm. I will give my life to protect it."

Nothing has ever felt more right than this.

Chapter 29
Cat

I find Vlad and Stefan in the yard, underneath the big oak tree. I rush over to them, waving to a few other people as I pass them by. As I approach them, Stefan turns around first and notices me. He immediately brightens up, and I can't help but be certain that it's all because of me. Vlad grins at me, and waves.

"Hey, hot stuff," he is the first one to say hi, as usual. He'd never allow someone else to beat him to it.

"Hey, guys," I reply feeling strangely awkward, despite everything that's happened between us.

Being a wolf is so much easier than being a human. There are different rules to follow, and you have to find the right words to express exactly what you're feeling. When you're a wolf, all you need to do is feel. Your instinct takes care of everything else.

"How are you feeling?" Stefan wonders.

I inhale deeply, then smile. "I have no idea where to start processing all the things, but I'm getting there."

"You really kicked ass back there, you know that?" Vlad lifts his hands up into the air, his fingers curling into fists, then starts hitting the empty air with them. "The way you punched Kaige, watched him move, then bit into him. And finally, the last blow. You left him to live. I think that was what hurt him more than any death ever could."

"Those were my thoughts exactly," I nod, feeling strangely pleased with myself.

"I really enjoyed it," Vlad continues with a grin. "So, now what?"

I sigh. "That's exactly what Taarus asked me a few hours ago."

"What did you tell him?" Stefan asks, curiously, tilting his head to take a better look at me.

I glance at him, then at Vlad. Their eyes are full of love. I can see it clearly. I want to stay. I know that now. But, what about them. Do they want to stay here, with me? Or will we need to separate and ache for the rest of our lives because of our bond that can never be broken?

I take a seat between them, on a little bench. Vlad puts his hand on my thigh, and I immediately feel the heat of his touch. My mind and my body remember their words, their breaths. I know I want more of that. So much more. But, for that, they need to stay. Only, I can't ask them to or order them. They have to stay with me because they want to.

"I am a silver white," I say, knowing full well that they've seen me. They know who I am. They also know what I am. "I am the guardian of the book of Thoth. Taarus has been guarding it long enough. He is old. And, I mean this in the nicest way possible – "

Vlad chuckles at my words, interrupting me. Stefan gives him a stern look, and Vlad immediately presses his lips together, preventing himself from chuckling again.

"So, as I was saying," I continue with a smile, already endeared by these two guys. I doubt I could live without either one of them. I need them both to be truly happy, because they both provide different things for me. They reach a different part of me. "Taarus just asked me, while it was up to me to make that decision for myself."

"Taarus would never impose his will upon anyone," Stefan adds.

"Exactly," I nod. "That is why his advice is all the more valuable. After speaking to him, I've realized that I don't want to leave this place."

I pause, because I'm not sure how the guys will take it. I have made that decision for myself. They have to make it on their own.

"I want to keep the book safe. I want to make sure that the Hermitage keeps being a safe haven for those who were once like us: unwanted outcasts who have nowhere else to go. I also know that there will always be more shifters like Kaige, those who believe they have the right to take what is not theirs to take. That is why I need to be here and protect not only the book, but this place and everyone in it."

I bite my lower lip, looking down at Vlad's hand still on my thigh. I wait for their reply, but neither of them speaks. Not yet. I dare not lift my gaze at either of them, because I'm afraid they will tell me what I don't want to hear. They might tell me that they've had enough time here, that they want to go out and explore the world. I can't do that. My place is here, with or without them.

All of a sudden, Stefan stands up. Vlad pulls his hand almost immediately and follows his brother. They still don't speak. Instead, I see Stefan offering me his hand, and I stand up, too.

I'm trembling, feeling like my heart is out of my chest, and with one single word, it might get broken into a million little pieces, never to be put together again. But, that is the price I'm willing to pay, as I wait for their decision to make my life into a fairy tale or a mere survival.

"When we bonded with you," Stefan starts, cupping my chin with his fingers and lifting my head to meet his gaze, "we promised ourselves to you. The female mate is by far the more important one in a bonded relationship."

I feel my cheeks flushing, something I'm not prone to, but hearing him speak this way makes me feel giddy and ecstatic.

"If it is your decision to stay, then we stay with you," he concludes as if it's the most natural thing to do.

"But, I don't want you to agree to it, just because of me," I shake my head. "What if you aren't happy here? What if you – "

This time Vlad interrupts me. "We are happy if you are happy."

"I..." I start, overwhelmed by their love.

"You are the most important person in our life," Vlad continues. "We've realized how important you are. I mean, we've suspected ever since you arrived here, but we had no idea you were a silver white. It is actually us who are not worthy of you."

"Not worthy!?" I almost shout, and a few people not far from us turn to see what's going on.

I just wave at them a little awkwardly smiling, then I turn my attention back to the guys.

"That's not true," I shake my head. "I'm no more special than you are."

"According to ancient legends, you are," Stefan reminds me. "There is no denying that, and it's alright. We know who we are. We also know who you are. If you accept us as you see us, then we shall be yours for the rest of our lives, to be lived here, at the Hermitage, helping you keep the place and the book safe."

"Stefan..." I feel my voice trembling. "Vlad..."

Before I can say anything else, they wrap their arms around me.. Vlad hugs me from the front, while Stefan wraps his arms around my waist. I inhale their scent deeply, feeling it soothe me to my very core. I've never felt this loved, this accepted, as I do now.

Hearing them say they will follow me anywhere and that they will stay by my side no matter what fills me with joy beyond measure.

I feel my wolf inside of me. Her energy is complete, effortless, in tune with my own. Our hearts are beating together, as one.

"You can always count on us for anything," Vlad whispers. "We love you more than you could ever imagine, although we may not know the best way to always show it. Especially Stefan."

Stefan immediately growls, but we all end up chuckling together, still intertwined in one big bear hug.

"You are loved more than you know, Cat," Stefan takes over, and I close my eyes, assured that I am finally where I belong.

My purpose has been fulfilled. Now, it is time to grab hold of my destiny, with Vlad and Stefan by my side. I lean onto Vlad, listening to the soft beating of his heart.

My heart.

Our hearts.

Epilogue
Cat

Five years later

It is still early in the morning. Willow has sent us all out of the dining room. She needs to clean up and get ready for the special early dinner we are to have. It is the celebration of the full moon, when the goddess of nature herself will bestow her graces upon us. It is an old custom, one that is rarely upheld nowadays. But, somehow breathing life into old habits and customs seems to bring us even closer together.

I walk outside into the yard. That is, I waddle, because I'm all belly. My dress tightens underneath my newly budding chest, then falls downward to my ankles, completely unable to hide my bulging belly. Not that I have any intention of hiding it. In fact, our unborn baby seems to be a wonderful source of joy at the Hermitage.

I still remember Willow's joy, and her kind words. Children are the saviors. We need more of them here, at the Hermitage. I myself cannot save the world or this place, but I sure can try.

I place my hands on my belly, feeling the soft kicks of the baby, who seems to love doing summersaults in there, not caring one bit that it's kicking my ribs in the process. I tap my belly gently with the tips of my fingers. She immediately responds.

She.

I'm almost certain it is a she. But, before I can whisper silently to her how eagerly I'm awaiting her arrival, I see the guys in the distance. They have been tending to the new part of the garden for the past few weeks, and the improvement has been noticeable.

Vlad notices me first. He stands up to wave. Then, he pats Rhain on the shoulder, and his curly little head turns around, noticing me. He waves excitedly, only to drop the shovel and the rake from his hands, then starts running to me with his arms stretched out.

"Mom!" I hear him shout in a voice that fills my heart with joyous love.

It takes only several pitter-patters of his little feet to reach me. I drop down to my knees, welcoming him into my arms. He buries his face into my neck. I inhale deeply, breathing in the soft scent of dirt and his washed hair.

I still remember the night he was born. The pain was unbearable, despite Willow's potions which she bade me drink. Sweat slid down my temples in long, hot streaks, and I felt like I was coming apart on the inside. She kept reminding me that pain is my friend. It means that my baby is separating from me, and with every wave of pain which passes through me, my baby is one step closer to being held in my arms. Those words soothed me, although I gritted my teeth through every contraction.

Willow would run out of the room then back with a fresh set of towels and clean water. I have no idea how long it lasted. Willow later told me it was about five hours in total, which supposedly isn't that long at all. I don't know. It felt like five whole days of pain, although I did focus all my attention on the arrival of my little darling.

Vlad couldn't take it. He would leave the room, then come back. But, when the time finally came, he looked away. Stefan held my hand the whole time. His hand would caress my cheek and wipe my forehead. At one point, I believed he'd need to tend to both me and Vlad, because Vlad got so pale seeing the head start popping out.

When Rhain was finally born, I could hear the soft tapping of rain outside. I knew right then and there what my firstborn son's name would be. Now, as I hold him in my arms, with even more love than on that first night of his arrival into this world, I know that the name suits him. There is a soft soothing energy inside of him, the kind of rain which eases the suffering of dry earth after a long period of draught. However, there is also a tempest inside of him, the likes of which could destroy an entire house or create a flood that would destroy everything in its path.

He is still too little to understand what all that means. He is a silver white, just like me. From what Taarus has told me, he will be even more powerful than I am. I'm not sure if that is a good thing or a bad thing. Maybe it's both. It's the kind of thing you need to balance out properly from early on. But, controlling him isn't always that easy.

Still, his kind nature is undeniable. His chocolate curls frame his face as he pulls away from my hug and presses his hand to my belly.

"How is the baby?" he wonders, smiling widely and showing me all of his slightly uneven teeth.

"Wonderful, thank you, darling," I smile back. "And, how is my big baby?"

He frowns at being called that. "I'm not a baby. I'm a big boy."

"Oh, I'm terribly sorry," I pretend to zip up my mouth, and it makes him chuckle. "I meant no offense, mister. I know you are a big boy."

"That's better," he nods importantly, and I pinch his cheek in reply.

"So, what have you been up to?" I wonder, lifting my gaze only to see Vlad and Stefan approaching us.

All three of them are dirty and dusty, but that is how I like my men.

"We've been putting up the fence around the vegetable patch," Rhain explains. "So, now it's all nicely separated."

"That sounds like a really professional job," I give him an appreciative nod back.

At that moment, Vlad and Stefan approach me on each side, and both of them plant a soft kiss on either side of my face.

"You are glowing," Vlad tells me.

"I feel like a balloon about to pop," I frown.

"No, you are like the sun," Vlad corrects me.

"As big as the sun?" I chuckle.

He pretends to frown. "Accept a damn compliment, woman."

Immediately, Rhain points his little finger at him. "Tata Vlad cursed."

"Why, yes," I lift my eyebrow at him importantly. "Yes he did."

"That means he helps Willow with the dishes tonight," Rhain cleverly remembers the rule about cursing we've employed, which Willow has welcomed with open arms.

"Tonight?" Vlad gasps. "But, it's the night of the festival. Come on!"

"You'll have a lot of work to do," I chuckle.

"Oh, come on," he shakes his head again, and all four of us burst out into boisterous laughter.

I turn to both of them, wrapping my arms around their necks and kissing them gently on the lips. Holding them both close, one then the other, makes all the tangled-up emotions inside of me clear up. The years we've spent here have been blissful. I know that it is just a matter of time before someone like Kaige tries to take the book again, and we shouldn't let our guard down, but I can't help but be focused on my family. My beautiful family, which has risen out of the darkest moment of my life, only to bring me up again and show me that life is truly worth living if you have someone to share it with.

Revenge has brought me little pleasure. When I stood over Kaige's weakened body, I knew that killing him would not satisfy me, nor would it respect the memory of my father's life. I refused to stoop down to his level. We've heard word of his life somewhere else, somewhere far away from here. I doubt he would ever dare come back, but even if he does, we would be ready for him, even more ready than we used to be.

For the time being, life is good. In fact, it is even better than good. I look at Vlad, at Stefan, at Rhain. I place my hands on my belly. I live for them. I don't live for myself any longer, and the thought fills me with joy. I caress Rhain's beautiful face. I never even dreamed I could be blessed with so much happiness.

The love we all feel for each other is burning brighter than any flame, and there isn't power strong enough in this world to extinguish it.

Suddenly, a tear rolls down my face. I lift my hand to wipe it away. This is no time for crying, even if it's tears of joy.

"Cat?" Vlad is the first one to notice it. "Are you OK?"

"What's the matter?" Stefan immediately follows up with his own question.

Even Rhain lifts his head up at me, curious as to why they were asking me this.

"I'm fine," I smile. "Really. I just feel so blissfully, overwhelmingly happy and I don't know what to do with myself," I chuckle.

Vlad leans over to me and kisses the tear away. Love's healing power lights up the world around us, and I know that I have made the right choice. This is where I need to be. This is where I belong, now and forever more.

*****

Enjoy what you read? Please leave a review!